NO FEAR!

Stephanie Perry Moore

NO FEAR!

Morgan Love Series
Book 5

MOODY PUBLISHERS
CHICAGO

All Scripture quotations are taken from the *New American Standard Bible*®, copyright © 1960, 1962, 1963, 1968, 1971, 1972, 1973, 1975, 1977, 1995 by the Lockman Foundation. Used by permission. (www. Lockman.org)

Edited by Kathryn Hall
Interior design: Ragont Design
Cover design and image: TS Design Studio
Author photo: Bonnie Rebholz
Word searches by Pam Pugh

Some definitions found at the end of chapters are from WordSmyth.net.

Library of Congress Cataloging-in-Publication Data

Moore, Stephanie Perry.
  No fear! / Stephanie Perry Moore.
    p. cm. -- (Morgan Love series ; #5)
  Summary: Morgan is worried about of a number of things—her father being in the war, a big test in school, having to tell a judge about being attacked by an older girl, and the death of one of her friends in an accident—but when her mother explains to her about God and heaven Morgan understands why she need not be afraid. Educational exercises provided at the end of each chapter.
  ISBN 978-0-8024-2267-5
  [1. Fear—Fiction. 2.Worry—Fiction. 3.Schools—Fiction.
4. Christian life—Fiction. 5. African Americans—Fiction.] I. Title.
PZ7.M788125No 2011
[Fic]—dc22

                              2011000094

Printed by Bethany Press in Bloomington, MN – 06/11

               1 3 5 7 9 10 8 6 4 2

Printed in the United States of America

For
My Maternal Aunt
Joann Roundtree Jefferson
(Born October 28, 1967)

When I was the main character's age, you were right
there with me. Growing up together you were my aunt
and my sister. Thank you for showing me what "no fear"
looks like. Your strength in the face of adversity is
remarkable. I hope every person reading this book lives
like you and knows that while going through anything
scary, have no fear—because God is there!

Contents

Chapter 1

Serious Stuff

"Okay, everybody, it's time to have a party!" Billy stood in front of the class and yelled. He had watched Mrs. Hardy after she stepped out of the room. By now she was already at the other end of the hallway.

Mrs. Hardy was headed to the principal's office. You didn't have to tell my classmates twice that it was time to have a bit of fun. Trey went up to our teacher's desk and turned on the radio. Sometimes she let us listen to it after our work, but it was never set to the station Trey had on. And it was never so loud either. I had a bad feeling that we were going to get in major trouble because of all this.

Brooke jumped up and reached her hand out to me. "Come on, Morgan. Let's dance!"

I wasn't trying to be a party pooper. I just knew we were supposed to be reviewing the last couple of weeks before Christmas break. The big standard test was coming in the spring.

Yeah, Mrs. Hardy got called away to the office, which is on the other side of the floor. But who could say that we wouldn't get caught? She was known for sneaking up and catching people doing stuff they weren't supposed to be doing.

Brooke and I had just talked about being each other's friend. We had such an on-again, off-again friendship. This time we promised we were going to help each other do the right things. So I gave Brooke a look like, *No, Brooke. Don't dance around the room and get in trouble like everybody else.*

But Brooke was already up, and I could see it in her eyes that she was ready to have some fun. Even so, I wasn't going to fall for that this time. I just sat there, looking at her with my hands on my hips.

Finally, I grabbed my best friend by her long ponytail and said, "We are not doing this, okay?" To my surprise, she didn't even argue with me and just sat down.

After a few minutes of watching the other kids, Brooke was becoming upset. "See that, Morgan? We could've been havin' fun too. Mrs. Hardy isn't even back yet."

Alec heard what she said and called out to us, "Yeah, but the ones she catches are gonna be in trouble!"

"Come on, Alec, man. Have a little fun," Trey said, as he bobbed up and down like a jumping jack toy.

Alec didn't back down. "We're gonna have fun. Whenever she gets back, it'll be time for recess. But the way you all are actin', you'll make sure we won't have any more free time this year."

"What are you doing? Are you about to tell on us?" Trey asked Alec, as Alec gently opened the classroom door and peeked out.

"No, I'm watchin' out for Mrs. Hardy since nobody's thinkin' about that," Alec said, sounding like the grown-up one.

"Good lookin' out, Alec! Party over here," Billy sang out, waving his hand around in the air.

I was really happy that Billy wasn't sad like he'd been acting lately. He and his sister and his mom had been living with his mom's aunt, Miss May. She was my grandmother's best friend and neighbor. Of course, since I wasn't an adult, they didn't tell me everything that was going on. But I think Billy's sister had been acting out because she was tired of moving around. My mom told me that some people just don't handle changes very well.

I know for myself that moving around a lot is a big deal. I remember when my parents got divorced and I had to move with my mom to a place I didn't know anything about. Once she got remarried, I moved back in with my dad. But then he got assigned to a naval ship off the coast of Africa to serve our country. When my dad left, I was so sad. At that time I had to go to a new school and move in with my mom, my new baby brother, Jayden, and Daddy Derek.

Since then, we haven't moved around anymore. I actually enjoy living with my new family. So everything turned out to be good after all. I was hoping the same would happen for Billy's family. But for now, I was just happy to see Billy smiling.

"Here she comes! Here she comes!" Alec yelled out and ran back to his seat.

Trey didn't listen. He kept the music going and half of the class didn't even sit down. None of them knew how close she was, and they didn't listen to what Alec said. They just kept doing the wrong thing.

"What in the world?" Mrs. Hardy said, as she walked in and **flicked** the lights on and off. "Who turned on that music?"

Suddenly, the class was silent. I sunk down in my seat because I didn't want her to call on me. If she did, I was going to have to tell and I didn't want to. I planned to keep still and to keep my mouth shut.

"You know what? I don't even want the answer. All of you students need to understand that this is not a time for play. I know Christmas is coming and you all are excited, but we have some important work to do. So, everybody settle down and let's get started."

I was so glad that she wasn't going to punish the whole class this time. Mrs. Hardy was a very smart lady and she knew what she was doing.

"First of all," Mrs. Hardy said, "the name of the standard test is the CRCT. Can anyone tell me what CRCT stands for?"

No one answered. Then Alec raised his hand. "Mrs. Hardy, I think CRCT stands for Criterion-Referenced Compare Test. I asked my brother Antoine about it because he had to take when he was in the third grade."

"The word is not compare, Alec. It is **competency**, but that was very close," Mrs. Hardy said.

"That sounds so confusing. I see why they just call it the CRCT," Brooke added.

Mrs. Hardy went on to tell us more about it. "The test is very important because it's going to tell how much you know. It is organized by subject and the content is based on the standards given by the state. The main purpose is to let parents know if their child understands the material they are being taught. Furthermore, it's important that you pass the CRCT in the spring so you can go on to the fourth grade. If you do not pass the reading and math, you will have to repeat the third grade and possibly be in my class again next year. Now, how many of you want that to happen?"

No one raised their hand. I don't think any of us wanted to be in the same grade over again just because we weren't ready to take that test. Our friends would pass us by while we're still in Mrs. Hardy's class, learning the same things and doing the same things all over again. For me, I was going to do my best not to let that happen.

"I know that all of you are more than able to pass the CRCT. However, the conduct that I saw just now from some of you makes me think you won't like your test results."

The more Mrs. Hardy kept talking, the more we started feeling smaller than ants. I hadn't even done anything but I was shaking. Just the thought of not passing that test and having to repeat a grade made my hands sweat and my heart beat faster. As Mrs. Hardy said, if we had to take the test today, I knew I wouldn't do well. At the moment, I was really afraid that I wouldn't pass the third grade.

Because of all this, I didn't think we should have recess. But Mrs. Hardy asked us why she should care to give us extra work since we didn't seem to care about passing the CRCT. I wanted to stay in my seat and ask her to teach us, please! But she made us line up to go outside and play. And off we went.

During recess, Trey came over to Brooke and me. "What's wrong with you, Morgan? Why are you lookin' at me like you're mad?"

"Mrs. Hardy said we need to make this time count for something and now she doesn't even wanna teach us because she thinks y'all were playin' too much."

Alec walked over bouncing a basketball. Trey said to him, "Alec, tell her we have plenty of time to get this. If we let ourselves worry too much, then we'll all be too scared to do a good job."

"Yeah, that's true. We can't take it too serious, but we do need to take it serious enough so we have the skills to pass," Alec replied. Then he took a shot at the net, making it with a *swoosh* sound.

"And what are you worried about anyway?" Trey asked

me. "You're gonna do better than any of us."

Alec started coughing. "I guess I see a contest comin' on."

"He's probably gonna do way better than me. I'm scared."

"You're scared, Morgan? Then I should be scared." I could tell Trey was starting to think about it all.

"What? You really don't think we're gonna pass?" asked Billy. "My sister said part of it was pretty hard . . . but we still have some time before we take it. Right?"

"Well, I'm just worried about repeating a grade, okay?" I said to my friends before walking off the playground. I was pretty much in tears.

• • • • •

"Derek, you're going to have to tell the church that you can't be there this time. You know that I have a house to show and you said you would be here this time when Morgan comes home. Can't you reschedule?" my mom asked, looking unhappy.

"But, honey," Daddy Derek said, "we agreed that my job takes **precedence**. Someone else in your office can show those clients around."

Mom stopped chewing and let her fork hit the table. She was pretty upset, but Daddy Derek wasn't about to give up. The two of them kept talking about it, with both of them giving their points of view. I don't know if they had forgotten that I was sitting at the dinner table or not. I was just feeling so lost. I heard what they were saying, but I didn't care and I wasn't really taking it all in anyway.

I had a standard test to get ready for. I needed to study for it because I could not fail. The whole idea was really scaring me. Because Mrs. Hardy kept telling us how important the results would be, nothing else was on my mind. Not even eating my favorite meal that was right before me. How could I not enjoy this large plate of spaghetti and juicy meatballs?

Today had just been hard. I didn't even want to play with my friends at recess. And, by no fault of my own, now I was listening to adults talk. I don't know why they were acting like I wasn't sitting right there.

"Can I be excused?" I finally said, after just playing around with my spaghetti.

Both of my parents looked at my plate and then looked at me. Mom said, "Morgan, you didn't even touch your food besides moving it from one side to the other. What's going on?"

"We're not angry with each other, if that's what you think, Morgan," said Daddy Derek.

I didn't want them to worry about me. They had their own problems. My mom had just started her new job. Although Daddy Derek thought he wanted her to work, it had been causing problems ever since. I certainly didn't want to throw my **anxiety** over the test in the mix.

"I just have some homework I need to look over. And I'm not that hungry."

"Morgan, please eat a little more, okay?" Mom requested.

Then Daddy Derek said, "Honey, why don't you just call your parents and have them sit over here until Morgan gets home?"

"Because they have something to do tomorrow and you said you were going to be here. I really have a problem with that."

"I can be here by myself," I said, surprised that those words just came out of my mouth.

"That's not a bad idea. At her age, she should be able to stay home by herself after school for a while. We should try it."

Mom just shook her head. She wasn't even trying to think about it. I guess I didn't like the fact that my mom still looked at me like her baby.

I spoke up, "Mom, I can do it. I'll be okay."

"I'll be home an hour and a half after she gets here. I just can't be here right away," Daddy Derek said. "If she's willing to try it and nothing is wrong with it, I think we should let her."

"Morgan, I have to tell you to eat all of your food. You're not ready to be here by yourself yet. It's not that I don't think you're a big girl, sweetheart. I just don't think it's time for you to be home alone right now."

I stood up from my chair and yelled, "That's so unfair!"

"Morgan, sit back down. You need to check your attitude, young lady."

She didn't have to tell me twice because I already knew

that having an A+ attitude was way better than having a rude one. It's just that sometimes when you don't get your way, it's hard to hold back your feelings.

"Mom, I'm sorry you think I have the wrong attitude, but I'm tryin' to grow up and you won't let me. I don't want anything else to eat, so can I please be excused? Please?"

"Go ahead, Morgan. I'll be there in a little while to talk to you."

Walking to my room, I prayed, *Lord, please help me keep my feelings in check. Mom and Daddy Derek are the parents and they know what's best for me. It's just that I get told no when I really wanna do something. Help me to understand that when I don't get my way it's okay. And help me not to be so afraid. In Jesus' name. Amen.*

I finished praying and put on my nightclothes for bed. Just then I watched my door slowly open and Mom creep in. I might as well be ready for the major letdown of not staying home by myself. So I was just waiting for her to tell me who my sitter was going to be for that time.

"Morgan, may I have a hug?" she whispered.

I had no problem giving her one. I had just prayed and asked God to help me not to be angry with her.

"You're growing up on me, sweetheart. I'll call as soon as you get off the bus. And Derek said he'll be here not too long after you get home."

"Oh, my goodness, Mom! You mean you're gonna let me?"

"Now, I need you to understand that this is a big deal, Morgan. I want you to lock the doors behind you right away. And you need to turn on the alarm as soon as you get in. The only thing I want you to make is a peanut butter and jelly sandwich because I don't want you cooking anything."

"I know, Mom. I know."

"Okay, then the answer is yes."

"Thank you, Mom!"

"Just don't make me sorry about it, Morgan."

"Yes, ma'am, I won't," I said in a serious tone, as I gave her a big kiss on the cheek.

• • • • •

"What's up, Morgan? You're night and day from the way you were yesterday," Brooke said to me when I walked into the classroom with my head held high and a smile **plastered** on my face.

"That's because I'm not a little kid anymore," I said.

Billy jumped in, "Well, the last time I checked, you were in third grade just like the rest of us."

"See, it's like this. Kids need someone to pick them up from the bus stop. Kids have to have someone with them when they get home from school. Some kids have to wait after school for their parents to pick them up, but big kids—like me—get to stay home alone," I said with pride.

Trey started laughing. "What! You're gonna stay home alone? Miss Chicken?"

"I won't be home alone for a long time and I'm not even supposed to tell people that I'll be home alone. But I'm growin' up and I'm proud of it."

Brooke walked up close and put her arm around me. "Are you sure you wanna stay home alone?"

"Yes, I'm sure. My mom trusts me and I don't wanna let her down. I'm ready for this."

Trey said, "Are you even old enough to stay by yourself?"

"You're gonna be like Dorothy on the *Wizard of Oz*," Billy added, "afraid of lions and tigers and bears."

Then Trey sneaked up behind me and shouted, "Oh my!"

Even though I jumped when he did that, I said, "I watched the *Wiz*! I'm not gonna be scared."

"Plus, you can call me if somethin' happens," said Alec.

"Oooh, you can call Alec," Billy teased.

"I'm not gonna call anybody. You guys are supposed to be my friends. Believe I can do this. Okay? And stop tryin' to scare me."

"Well, you were our friend yesterday until you said we were all gonna fail the CRCT," said Billy.

"I'm sorry about that."

"I'm just sayin', if you're scared to take a little test, you're certainly gonna be scared to be home by yourself. As soon as you hear a little noise, you'll be jumpin' around the house, tryin' to hide somewhere. Don't say I didn't warn you. Besides, I think you have to be in the fourth grade before you're allowed to stay by yourself," said Mr. Know-It-All Trey.

"Okay, class, sit down. It's time to start the day." Mrs. Hardy called us to attention. "Morgan, Alec, you two need to get your things and get on the Challenge bus. You have a morning session today."

After Alec and I got a seat on the bus, I asked him, "Do you think I'm too young to stay home by myself? You think I can do it, right?"

"Don't let anybody make you afraid. I like the strong Morgan who's cool about things and not easily **persuaded**. Stop sweatin' it. You're gonna find trouble if you keep lookin' for it."

Alec was right. I did have lots of doubts about every-thing. But the rest of the day went by too fast, and I wasn't ready to go home yet. And I was becoming more afraid of the lions and tigers and bears—even though I knew they weren't at my house. Billy and Trey had frightened me for sure.

Before I knew it, I was at my door, ready to go in. I reached into my book bag to pull out the key. As soon as I began to turn the knob, it started to thunder. No way did I wanna be outside, so I quickly pushed open the door and stepped inside. When I shut the door, the security alarm seemed to sound louder than it does when Mom or Daddy Derek come home. I rushed over to turn it off before the police came to see about me.

Everything seemed strange to me. The whole house looked extra dark. I knew it was because it was cloudy outside, but I was really scared! What if someone was waiting for me around the corner or down the hallway? Right away, I started thinking that someone would try and come in.

I should have felt safe, right? Wrong. The thunder I heard as I was coming in the door was just a warm-up because it got louder and louder. The rain was coming down hard and beating against the windows. I wanted to turn on the TV to drown out the noise, but I remember Mama telling me not to use the electricity when the weather was like this. I also thought about my friend Billy getting hit by lightning, so I was trying to play it cool.

The only thing I could do was sit in a ball and rock back and forth, praying,

"Okay, Lord, I'm scared. I need You to help me calm down. This wasn't a good idea for me to be home alone after all. I don't wanna be afraid, Lord."

The phone rang and I jumped. What if it wasn't Mom or Daddy Derek? What if it was someone I didn't know who knew I was home by myself and they were coming to get me? I was making up all kinds of scary **scenarios**, and none of this was good for me. I ran into my parents' room to get the phone and then the ringing stopped. As soon as it started back again, I quickly picked it up.

"Hello? Hello?"

I finally heard a welcome voice. "Morgan, are you okay, sweetheart?"

"Mama, please come and get me! I'm scared. It's thundering and lightning." The sky seemed like it was falling on the house! "I'm hearing all kinds of noises."

"Calm down, girl. Papa and I are pulling onto your street right now. We'll see you in just a minute."

Before I knew it, my grandparents were standing at the front door. I turned off the alarm and flung the door open, wrapping my arms around both of them so tight.

"I told you we needed to be close by. I knew it wasn't a good idea for her to be home by herself," Mama said.

"Yeah, but it's good we let her try. It's all this lightning and storming that got her worried," said Papa.

"I was so wrong. I shouldn't have wanted to be home by myself," I said, as I tried to calm down.

Papa took my hand and said, "I'm going to teach you Psalm 23. Say this with me, 'The Lord is my shepherd, I shall not want. He makes me lie down in green pastures; He leads me beside quiet waters. He restores my soul; He guides me in the paths of righteousness for His name's sake. Even though I walk through the valley of the shadow of death, I fear no evil, for You are with me; Your rod and Your staff, they comfort me. You prepare a table before me in the presence of my enemies; You have anointed my head with oil; my cup overflows. Surely goodness and lovingkindness will follow me all the days of my life, and I will dwell in the house of the Lord forever.'"

"Basically, it says we should have no fear," Mama explained.

Something was going on with me and I was confused. I wanted to act older, but I was nervous about everything. Even so, I couldn't let my fears defeat me. Like Papa said, I had to remember the words to Psalm 23 because being afraid of everything just wasn't the right way to be. This was serious stuff.

Letter to Dad

Dear Dad,

It was a bad storm and the lights scared me when they flicked off and on. I was home alone because Mommy's job took precedence over her being home this afternoon. I thought I was old enough to be home alone, but I'm not ready yet. I'm a little nervous about a lot of stuff.

Dad, I've got major anxiety about the test we're gonna take soon. "Not wanting to take the competency test" is plastered all across my face. Mama and Papa persuaded me to trust God and have no fear. But I need you to pray for the standard tests I have to take soon because the scenarios I have of failing them are creepier than that spider that crawled on me when I was five.

Your daughter,
Scared Morgan

Word Search

```
I  N  D  I  A  N  A  S  E  N  O  J
M  X  C  Q  S  R  I  T  X  A  D  C
P  P  R  E  C  E  D  E  N  C  E  A
O  E  B  Z  E  Y  W  P  H  O  R  L
R  R  G  S  N  S  A  H  W  M  E  I
T  S  J  H  A  P  L  E  M  P  T  F
A  U  S  A  R  A  K  N  G  E  S  O
N  A  F  L  I  C  K  E  D  T  A  R
T  D  U  T  O  E  L  N  V  E  L  N
M  E  R  U  S  N  O  R  E  N  P  I
T  D  R  H  A  R  D  Y  P  C  O  A
K  E  Y  T  E  I  X  N  A  Y  F  D
```

ANXIETY

COMPETENCY

FLICKED

PERSUADED

PLASTERED

PRECEDENCE

SCENARIOS

Words to Know and Learn

1) **flick** (flĭk) *verb*
To burn or shine unsteadily, such as a light.

2) **com·pe·ten·cy** (kŏm'pĭ-tən-sē) *noun*
Ability.

3) **prec·e·dence** ('pre–sə–dənts) *noun*
Priority.

4) **anx·i·e·ty** (ăng–zī'ĭ–tē) *noun*
A state of uneasiness.

5) **plas·ter** (plăs'tər) *verb* **plas·tered** (past tense)
To smear a surface with a coating of some kind.

6) **per·suade** (pər–swād') *verb* **per·suad·ed** (past tense)
To cause to believe something.

7) **sce·nar·i·o** (sĭ–nâr'ē–ō', –när'–, –năr'–) *noun* **sce·nar·i·os** (plural)
A made-up idea of what could happen.

Chapter 2

The Helper

"Okay, class, I need to talk to you about something serious."

It was the first day back to school after the Christmas break. Mrs. Hardy wasn't playing either. She had changed the desks around so that we weren't sitting by our friends anymore. She also had new rules on the board that meant she wasn't going to put up with anyone acting up in class.

It was countdown time! Our teacher had already told us only 118 more days until the CRCT. I had a huge lump in my throat, not at all wanting to take that hard test. There was no way around it, though.

Maybe if I prayed every day until the big test, the Lord would help me get through it. So I prayed silently, *Lord, the standard test is the serious thing our teacher wants to talk to us about. I just need You to help me not be afraid.*

"Listen up, class. I'm not going to tell you all two or

three times to quiet down," Mrs. Hardy said, before I finished my prayer. "As some of you may know, the Super Bowl is coming up in a little while and the National College Football Game is coming soon too. I am a big football fan and so I'm saying to you, it's game time. Just like in the field of sports, we have to get ready to win. So when I say listen up, I don't need all of the little rumblings through the class. I need you all to pay attention."

Everyone got quieter than a kid playing hide-and-seek, not wanting to be found. Mrs. Hardy noticed it too, so she kept talking.

"Now, what I want to share with you today is the fact that we're getting a new student. This student will not be in our room all the time, but at least half of the time each day. He's not a brand-new student to our school. You all have seen him, but you haven't attended class with him on a daily basis."

We all looked around thinking, *Who is she talking about? What's the big deal?*

"Tim Clark is going to be our new student."

"That's the boy everybody was joking about," someone from the back of the room called out.

"And that's exactly why I wanted to talk to you before he comes in here today. There will be no more talk like that. I'm going to let it pass this one time, but not a second. I don't even want to know who said it. We are all special in one way or another. None of you are so smart that you don't need a teacher to help you pass this grade. And yes, though Tim is a special needs student, he's not alone. He's just different."

Billy raised his hand. "Why does he have to be in our class? We all might have special needs. But for real, Mrs. Hardy, people might tease him. Not because they're tryin' to be mean. It's because he does act different."

Mrs. Hardy's face got even more serious and I could tell she was getting very upset.

"I know this will be a growing experience for all of you. Learning how to accept people who are different is a big part of life. You will find that children like Tim have the same feelings as anyone else. Even though he has special needs, we all have the need to depend on others from time to time. That's why I plan to call on each of you at different times to assist me with teaching him. Many times when people pick on someone else, it's out of **ignorance** or fear. That's not how we're supposed to be. We're supposed to help each other in any way that we can."

Trey raised his hand. "I'm just sort of afraid of people like Tim. One time I helped out with my mom at a place for extra special people and they scared me."

"Trey, you know Tim," Mrs. Hardy said. "That is highly unlikely to happen."

"Yes, I know him. He's cool, but I'm just sayin'—"

"I just need you all to treat Tim like you would want to be treated. No one wants to be made fun of. Give him the same respect you would want. Is that understood?"

"Yes, Mrs. Hardy," we said together.

Shortly after our talk, the principal, Dr. Sharpe, knocked on our door and Tim came running in.

"Hey! Hey!" He darted behind Mrs. Hardy then stood still, moving back and forth in a **sporadic** manner.

"Tim, you're going to have to settle down. We go out for recess in a little while, but right now it's time for our lesson, okay?" Mrs. Hardy said to him.

"Yes, ma'am. Where do I sit? Where do I sit?" he asked, as he circled around her.

There was an empty seat next to me. I still felt like I owed Tim something. I hadn't forgotten Field Day from last year when I joined in with the crowd picking on him. He saw me making fun of him and got really upset. True enough, I got in trouble. But even worse than that, I made him feel bad. Although I made it up to him by asking the class to throw Tim a big party, I still felt like I needed to do more. I raised my hand to let Mrs. Hardy know that Tim could sit next to me.

"Thank you, Morgan. That is a good idea. Tim, come this way." She led him to the seat on my right.

Before Dr. Sharpe left the room, she said, "Class, I'm really proud of you all for making Tim feel welcome. Everyone has to pass the CRCT, and I expect you all to do your best. Mrs. Hardy is one of our top teachers, so with the great teaching you all are being **exposed** to, I'm sure I will see high marks soon."

"Yes, Dr. Sharpe, I'm going to give the class a practice test when we come back from recess," said Mrs. Hardy.

"They know more than they think."

As the two of them smiled at each other, I started to worry all over again. It was the first time I knew about a practice test. We had just gotten back to school from the Christmas break. She had given us study sheets to look over during the break, but I didn't do them because it was Christmas. I was pretty sure no one else did any studying either because everyone else was looking worried too. As my head started hurting, all I could do was put my hand up to my forehead. This was really scary stuff.

Tim saw me and touched my hand. "My friend, Morgan. You'll be okay. You can do the test. You'll be okay."

I took a deep breath. He was right, I could do it. I thought I was going to be the one helping Tim out, but just his kind words helped me so much.

● ● ● ● ●

"Okay, class. Let's line up for recess," Mrs. Hardy said.

Every step I took, Tim was two steps behind me. "I'm stayin' with you, friend Morgan. When I get outside I'm playin' kickball. Kickball me, kickball you!"

"I thought we were playin' dodge ball, Morgan," Brooke said. "Don't tell me we have to babysit this boy all of recess and for the rest of the year. Ugh!"

Tim might be different, but he was smarter than a lot of us thought. I guess we doubted him because he wasn't exactly like the rest of us. He heard what Brooke said and started shaking his head from side to side. "No dodge ball for me. Kickball. Friend Morgan play with me."

"You hurt his feelings," I said to Brooke. I thought she had a soft spot when it came to Tim, but he could tell Brooke didn't wanna play with him.

"I'm sorry," she said, looking down at the floor. She felt bad.

As we waited for our teacher to lead the way, we had to be silent in the halls. Tim was superexcited to be in our class and I was surprised that he was acting so cool. We were used to seeing Tim in the halls, skipping and jumping. He was all over the place sometimes, but today in our class he stood in line just like the rest of us.

As soon as we got outside, all of the kids ran to get a spot on the blacktop. There was a bin that had the balls in it, and the boys rushed over to get the best ones.

Trey called out, "Come on, Brooke. We're playin' dodge ball over here."

Tim was walking really slowly. I went to the bin and there was one ball left. I picked it up and held it out to him. "Kickball. Me and you?"

"Yes! Kickball! Me and friend Morgan!"

I saw a spot on blacktop where no one was playing. I thought it was best for Tim and me to be alone. I rolled the ball to him. He kicked it and then ran right to third base. I wasn't sure if I was supposed to tell him that you kick the ball, run to first base, second base, third base, and then to home base. Or maybe I should just let him play his way. So I stood there, scratched my head, and just watched him.

"You don't know what to do, do you?" I heard a voice say. I turned around and it was Alec. "I'll help you teach him how to play, if you want."

"You'd do that?" I asked. I was happy for his help, but a little surprised that Alec would be so nice to Tim.

"Yeah. I think it's kinda cool that you're not afraid of him," Alec said, telling me he approved.

"Well, he reminds me of my baby brother, honestly . . . Tim's just another person who needs help. And he tries really hard."

Alec said, "I just don't wanna mess up and upset him."

"You can't be too hard on yourself. Relax. Stay calm and he'll be calm. He doesn't want you to feel sorry for him."

"How do you know?"

"Because of the way Brooke acted toward him in the line. She said she was sorry, but he still didn't want to play with her. The only reason he'll play with you is if he thinks you really want to play with him."

"I do want to, but I want him to play the right way."

"Okay, then let's teach him."

Alec and I went over to Tim. "Hey, Tim, I want you to meet my friend, Alec."

"Ummm . . . no. I only play with friend Morgan. No boys. Boys are mean. Me and friend Morgan only."

"Tim," Alec said, "I know boys are sometimes mean to you. I'm not like that. If I'm mean to you, just come out and tell me. Okay?"

"Okay. New friend Alec! Alec! I'll play with Alec. Bye, Morgan!"

"Wait. Both of us want to play with you, Tim," I said to him.

"Really? Play with me? I can cry." Tim's eyes watered.

He hugged me as the three of us started to play together. It was a real hug and it felt good. This was better than when I eat Mama's brownies. I just felt all yummy on the inside.

I couldn't say that everybody liked me, because there were lots of times when I was by myself. Last year, I was alone much of the time at school. I guess I liked hanging with Tim because I knew what it felt like to be **isolated**.

Alec explained to Tim how to play the game. Since I'm not the best kickball player, I spent the time practicing how to kick the ball while Alec was giving Tim a lesson. Before I knew what was going on, Brooke, Trey, and Billy were coming over to us.

Trey said, "Can we play with y'all?"

"You'll have to ask Tim about that," I said to them. I knew that my new buddy liked to choose the kids he played with.

When they asked him, Tim got super excited. All of us could have played better, rolling the ball faster and kicking the ball harder. But my friends cared more about Tim being happy than they did about winning a game. So we rolled slower and kicked softer. Before long, the whole class was cheering Tim as they watched and some others joined the game. Tim was so happy that the class was playing with him. He was a part of it all. He was a star.

The sun was shining bright and I sort of felt like Jesus was saying, *You know what, Morgan? Good job!*

•••••

When it was time to line up and go inside, I wanted to stay outside and play. I wanted to pick up leaves that were stuck to the grass. I even wanted to watch ants crawl from blacktop to blacktop. I wanted to do anything that would keep me from going inside to take that practice test. Even if one of the questions was $1 + 1 = 2$, I was so **anxious** about it, I might put 10 for my answer. I knew I needed to get a handle on things. I could do this. But why did I feel I couldn't? Why was I so nervous?

When Mrs. Hardy let us take a washroom break, I said to Brooke, "I don't think I can pass."

"Why are you so afraid? You're the smartest girl in this class. My mom had me do some of the stuff over Christmas break on her computer. It's not even that hard. I know if I can do it, you can too."

I just had to be crazy. I thought no one did work during the holidays. Brooke had studied over the break? And she was more prepared than me? Something was wrong.

"Okay, class." Mrs. Hardy was ready for us to settle down. After she passed out the test papers, she said, "It's time to take a practice test. I want you to do your best. The first part is math and you will have thirty minutes to complete it. When I say pencils down, I want your pencils down and your hands in your lap. Now, turn your papers over and go."

When I turned over the test, the first questions were about adding like **denominators**.

$1/12 + 4/12 = $ ____.

Well, I knew you were supposed to add the 1 and the 4, which equals 5. Then I thought about adding the denominators which would be 24. But that seemed like too much. With fractions, if you have the same denominator, you keep it the same. But I had to guess. When I looked at the choices, one of the answers was 5/24, and another one was 5/12. I didn't know which was right, so I circled 5/24.

Next, I came to $11/12 + 5/12$.

Now I was really confused, because $11 + 5$ equals 16. Then I circled 16/24. This was getting harder.

The next problem was $10/11 + 1/11$. And I circled 11/22.

Later on after the test, we switched papers and graded each other's tests. The answer for $1/12 + 4/12$ is 5/12, not 5/24, because when the denominator is the same, you don't add the bottom numbers. The answer to $11/12 + 5/12$ is 1 1/3. I had no clue how that came about until Mrs. Hardy explained it.

"This one is a little tricky. What you do is always keep the denominator the same, so 12 is the bottom number. For the numerator, $11 + 5$ is 16. However, you have to find out how many times 12 goes into 16. The answer is one time, so you put the 1 out front as a whole number. What you have left is 4/12. But you can't leave it there. Some of you did and we'll work on that. The number 4/12 can be reduced down to 1/3. That's because 4 goes into 12 three times. So the full answer is 1 1/3."

I thought to myself, *Wow, how will I ever remember that?* But I was trying hard to keep up with Mrs. Hardy.

"Finally, with 10/11 + 1/11, you keep the denominators the same and add the numerators, which is 11/11. But anytime you have the same numerator and denominator, it equals what? Class?"

"One!"

"That's correct. It would not be 11/11; the answer is the whole number 1."

So then, I got all three in that section wrong. I wasn't happy about that at all. We moved on to grade the next part. And I didn't do any better with the English. The section was on **possessive** pronouns. Possessive pronouns take the place of a possessive noun. Instead of saying "Tracy's book," I could use the possessive pronoun and say, "her book."

The question was: I am going to see Jacob's new truck. I was confused again and got it wrong. Because of the *'s,* I put "their" truck instead of the right answer, which is "his" truck. The *'s* just meant it was Jacob's truck.

The next question was: Is that Mike and Sue's cat?

Because Mike was first, I thought it was "his" cat. Really, the answer was "their" cat because the cat belonged to two people. I needed to study more because I kept putting down the wrong answers.

The last question: Did you see the peacock's feathers?

This one was really tricky. I didn't know if the peacock was a boy or a girl. Instead of putting "its" feathers as my answer, I put "his." I was all over the place. I got so much wrong, it was scary to even look at my paper. I just threw down my pencil and put my head down on my desk.

Mrs. Hardy came over to me. "Morgan, what's wrong?"

"I'm going to fail the CRCT. I'm not gonna do well because I messed up on my practice test. I'm gonna be held back in the third grade, Mrs. Hardy."

"We just need to find out what you don't know and work on that. So when the real test comes, you'll be ready."

"But what am I supposed to do?"

"I'm going to recommend you get tutoring."

"Tutoring? I can't do tutoring. That's for kids who have trouble learning."

"Okay. You just told me that you really didn't know the right answers. I watched you mark wrong answers on your test. Now, you can either go to tutoring and get some help, or you can fail your test because you didn't understand and refused to get help."

I bowed my head and said quietly, "Yes, ma'am. I need to go to tutoring."

"Now, that's the right attitude. And, Morgan, you don't have to worry about what anybody says or thinks. It's about you understanding this material and knowing that you're smarter than you think. There's absolutely nothing wrong with staying after school to get extra help. You're always helping other people. Now it's time for you to let someone else be the helper."

Letter to Dad

Dear Dad,

You would have been proud of my class today. We got a new student named Tim. At first, I thought that **ignorance** was gonna be a problem because some of the kids didn't want him around. He acts differently and makes **sporadic** moves. But, when we were **exposed** to his heart, we all cared. No one wants to feel **isolated**. Tim gets anxious too but sometimes we all do. I imagine you get **anxious** on your ship sometimes.

Also, I've got to get a tutor to help me with my **denominators** and **possessive** nouns.

Your daughter,
Helper Morgan

Word Search

```
M E R S M D X V E N U S
C U E X P O S E D J R U
R Y N A Y O V E L O M P
S A T U R N R E T A A O
B I F O L D O A P N R S
E S B R I N N R D X S S
L O G K R I R T C I C E
O L H V M A E H Z O C S
N A K O B S H M E U O S
G T N S A T U R N S U I
E E C N A R O N G I D V
D D J U P I T E R J S E
```

ANXIOUS

DENOMINATORS

EXPOSED

IGNORANCE

ISOLATED

POSSESSIVE

SPORADIC

Words to Know and Learn

1) **ig·no·rance** (ĭg'nər-əns) *noun*
The state of being uneducated or uninformed.

2) **spo·rad·ic** (spə-răd'ĭk, spô-) *adjective*
Occurring at irregular intervals; having no pattern or order in time.

3) **ex·pose** (ĭk-spōz') *verb* **ex·posed** (past tense)
To allow an action, influence, or condition to be revealed.

4) **i·so·late** (ī'sə-lāt') *verb* **i·so·lat·ed** (past tense)
To set apart or cut off from others.

5) **anx·ious** (ăngk'shəs, ăng'shəs) *adjective*
Uneasy; worried.

6) **de·nom·i·na·tor** (dĭ-nŏm'ə-nā'tər) *noun*
The part of the fraction below the division line.

7) **pos·ses·sive** (pə-zěs'ĭv) *adjective*
Showing ownership through grammar.

Chapter 3

Scary Thought

"So you think you're all that and too good to be in here, don't you?" the short girl with the cool hairdo said to me. Her name was Greta Ross.

Greta was in my regular class and she was also in my tutoring session. I don't know what made her think I felt like I was too good. Okay, maybe I was walking into the classroom looking worried but that's because I was a little fearful. Even so, that was no reason for her to think that way about me.

The truth is, I didn't want to get tutored because I didn't want to admit that I was scared to take the CRCT. Mrs. Hardy said that being in tutoring would help me get the help I needed to **excel** on the standard test. I just couldn't understand why Greta wanted to make this a hard time for me.

"Leave me alone," I told her. "I'm here to learn, not to fight with you."

"Ooh, well let me leave the little princess alone," she teased, as she turned her nose up at me.

This was so strange. She was in my class but that didn't mean we were around each other all the time. We never played at recess together. We never ate lunch together. We'd never even spoken to each other until today. Why was she speaking to me this way now? Mom told me that if you don't have anything nice to say, then don't say anything. Well, Greta didn't seem to know that rule. Maybe no one was teaching her how to be **refined**.

"That's okay. I'll leave you alone. You're always making us feel bad with your 99s and 100s. But you must not be too smart if you're in here with us," she huffed.

Now she was really making me upset. "Greta, I never said I was smarter than anyone else, did I?" I asked her.

She just looked at me and rolled her eyes. "We couldn't even get extra points on our last test because you scored so high. Most of us got 60s and 70s and Mrs. Hardy couldn't do anything to help us. 'No curve because of Morgan Love,'" Greta said, mimicking our teacher.

Not backing down, I stood my ground. "And that was my fault because I study hard? I study long before a test, not just the night before. I do more homework than she gives us and not just the problems she says to do. My studying pays off. That's all."

Greta said, "Huh! That's just another way of sayin'

you're better than the rest of us."

"It works the same way for anybody, Greta. If you wanna get good grades, you have to study hard, pray, and trust God to help you. Doing those things will make you feel smarter. My Papa told me that the Bible says a man is what he thinks he is. So don't even think that you're not smart, because you can be."

When I heard myself saying those words, I wondered why I was having some problems right now with the very same things.

"Well, don't think you know more than me, Morgan Love. There's lots that you don't know."

"Okay, I never said I knew everything either."

"You think you're better than me."

"How do I think I'm better than you?"

"You never talk to me. We don't sit together at lunch. We don't hang out at recess. One time when we were choosing partners for a science project, you saw me and turned your head away. Then you asked to be partners with Alec."

"First of all, I don't remember that. I don't eat with you or play with you because you never even come near me. A friendship goes two ways, you know. So you could talk to me sometimes. That's not fair for you to put all of that on me, Greta, like it's my fault."

I was getting emotional because I was thinking about my own fear of testing. "I'm down on myself. I do a lot of studying, but I could still fail. I'm in tutoring for a reason. I have to try real hard and I'm not sayin' that's anybody's fault. And you should say the same. I'm a cool person and I care about my friends. And just because we haven't been friends up to this point doesn't mean we can't start now."

When I was finished, Greta didn't come at me with a negative response. She didn't yell at me. She didn't roll her eyes. She just looked out the window like she was imagining us being friends.

We were still waiting for our teacher to come in, so we had extra time to talk to each other. I didn't want to argue with anyone though. Before the teacher showed up, I wanted to relax so that nothing would distract me from my lesson. So, I sat quietly and watched Greta, waiting for her to speak.

"Okay, I was wrong. We can be friends and we can study for the big test together. Right? What's your number?" she asked, pulling out her cell phone. As soon as I saw her cool phone, it reminded me of how I wished my folks would let me have one.

"I'll have my mom call your mom so they can make play dates for us. We'll be the best of friends," I told her.

"Just give me your number. What's the big deal?" She'd gone from being rude to being nice. Now she was being pushy.

I didn't want to set her off again, so I started writing on a piece of paper. "I'll give you my home number and we can start from there."

"Here's my number," she said, sliding a piece of ripped

notebook paper to me. "Greta Ross. Call me tonight. It has to be between five and seven. I won't get home until after five and I can't talk after seven. Okay?"

I didn't answer because just then the teacher walked in. I was both excited and thankful that she saved me from agreeing to something I wasn't sure about.

"Everybody, take a seat at the computers along the wall. If you put in your login and password, you can access the math practice tests. So let's get started."

I sat at the computer right next to Tim. When the results from my first practice came back, I hung my head low. Staring at the screen, I only got 6 out of 10 correct. I didn't even know that my eyes were getting watery until I saw Tim pull a tissue out of his pocket and hand it to me.

He knew how to encourage like the best cheerleader I'd ever seen. "It's okay, friend Morgan. You'll get this. Try more, try."

I didn't know what was going on with me. Maybe I wasn't thinking hard enough. Was I answering the questions too quickly? Did I really not know the answers? It felt good to hear Tim tell me it was gonna be okay. I had to start doing what I told other people to do. I told Greta that I worked hard for my grades. I told her that you are what you think you are. Think like a winner and you'll be a winner.

You can do this, Morgan Love. You can do this. I had to keep telling myself. *You are smart. You can answer these questions right, so there's no need to be anxious.*

I asked the tutor to explain the problems that I got wrong. She helped me go through them. Then I went back and took the math test over again. When I clicked "submit" to grade it, I had 8 out of 10 correct this time. Much better, but not where I wanted to be. It made me want to practice every day until I got them all right. But at least I was beginning to see that I could do this.

Tim saw my score and clapped for me. "Yay, friend Morgan!"

When I saw his test score of 7 out of 10, I said, "Yay, Tim!"

We both could do it and we did.

•••••

"I'm just **devastated**," Brooke said into the phone the next day after school.

Something was wrong with her. She sounded really upset. I wasn't sure if she was mad with me or something else was going wrong in her life. By her short and sassy tone, I was thinking that it was about me.

So, I asked her, "What's wrong?"

"Oh, like you don't know." Now I was sure it had something to do with me.

"What did I do now?" I asked a little snippily. I was tired of people making me feel like I'd done something when I hadn't.

"Well, when you were at Challenge today I had to listen to Greta Ross going on and on about you being her new best friend. She kept saying how you guys were gonna hang out, and I felt really left out. And you haven't been callin' me."

"I haven't been callin' her either, Brooke. I just got her number yesterday."

"That's not what she said."

What did she say? I wondered. And why would Brooke believe her without asking me about it first. And what was wrong with me calling Greta if I wanted to?

Brooke paused. "Okay, I don't know if she said you called her or if she called you, but she did say y'all have been talkin'."

"We talked in our tutoring session, but that's it. The only reason we talked then was because she wouldn't stop talking. I already have a best friend, Brooke. You know that."

Brooke softened her voice. "You really mean that?"

"I do, girl. You're my friend. You're my girl. We get each other. You should already know that Greta was only saying those things to make you jealous."

"Okay. Well, it's my own fault," Brooke said.

"Huh?" I said, kind of surprised because Brooke never took the blame for anything. Well, maybe sometimes, but not all the time.

"I mean, when you're away at Challenge, I talk to Greta. I don't wanna be around the boys all the time. And since she and I don't really have much else to say, I talk about you all day to her. I guess I made her jealous of our friendship and she wanted to throw that back in my face.

Even if you were her friend, you'd be the only one because she doesn't have any. She probably just needs a friend, and I don't want her to take my best friend away from me."

We laughed at that and it was good. All of a sudden, I heard a knock on our front door and then the doorbell rang. When I peered out the window, I was surprised to see a police car in the driveway.

"I gotta go, Brooke. We're good, right? Somebody's at the door and I need to go and tell my mom," I said, rushing her off the line.

"Your mom doesn't hear the doorbell?" Brooke asked, all in my family's business.

Sighing, I said, "She's under the hair dryer with rollers in her hair."

"Ooh, that's cool. She can do her own hair. I need to wash—"

I cut her off. "Brooke, I have to go! We're cool, right?"

"Yeah. I'm sorry I listened to what someone else was sayin'. I won't do that again."

"Bye, girl," I said into the phone.

"Bye."

I quickly went into the kitchen. Mom was still under the dryer, so I lifted the top and said, "Doorbell."

"Well, did you look out and see who's there?"

"Mom, it's a policeman."

"What? Okay. You stay right here. The baby must still be asleep. Have you been listening to the monitor like I told you? I'll be right back."

Before I could say anything else, Mom went to the door. And I stayed in the kitchen as I was told. *What's going on?* I wondered.

"It's a **subpoena** for you," Mom said when she returned to the kitchen.

I didn't know that word and it sounded kinda scary. "What does that mean?" I asked. She could tell that I was already fearful.

"Sit down, sweetie. A subpoena is when the judge calls you to testify against something or someone."

"What does testify mean?"

"It means you can be a witness and tell a judge about something another person did wrong."

"Well, why do I have a subpoena?"

"Let's see," she said, as she started to read the letter. "Oh, wow."

"Wow what? Tell me, Mom."

"It says they want you to be a witness against Bridget Wood."

"Why does she have to go to court?"

"It says that her stealing from you wasn't her first offense, so the school is pressing charges against her."

"What does pressing charges mean?" I asked, as my tummy started feeling uneasy.

Rubbing my back to calm me, Mom said, "When a person does something wrong, another person can bring the wrongdoer before a judge."

"But, Mom, Bridget confessed what she did wrong and

she apologized. She even let Jesus into her heart. If I testify against her, I would have to tell the truth. But I don't wanna have to stand in front of a judge and put my hand on a Bible and tell on Bridget."

"Well, you're right. When you're called to court, sweetie, you have to tell the truth. Remember what we told you? Sometimes a person's actions have consequences that they can't do anything about. They just have to accept their punishment."

Almost crying, I said, "But I don't wanna get anybody in trouble."

Being loving, but firm, Mom said, "You have to answer a subpoena, baby. You don't have a choice."

I was feeling so bad. My heart and head were pounding. I just felt sick all over. It felt worse than having the flu.

"Mommy, why?"

"I'm here with you, Morgan. Let's not panic."

I hoped she could get to the bottom of this and fix it. The thought of me going to court and telling on someone scared me pretty badly. Bridget already apologized for being mean to me. This was not a good feeling. She had learned her lesson and everything was gonna be okay. This was supposed to be over.

• • • • •

It was late and I couldn't sleep. My worry was getting the best of me. I thought about drinking some warm milk. When I was little, Mom would give it to me after I had a bad dream. I would drink it and go fast asleep. That's what I needed right now.

I put on my slippers and headed to the kitchen. As I walked softly past my parents' bedroom so that I wouldn't wake them, I heard Mom's voice. She was crying. Now I was even more scared. Their door was open, so it wasn't like I was listening on purpose. I thought about going in, but I just stood there. I had to figure out what was going on with my mom.

Mom cried out, "Oh, my goodness, Derek. How am I ever going to tell her if this is true? An attack on a ship? Morgan can't handle this. Not her dad."

"It'll be okay, honey. If it is his ship, we'll get her through it," I heard Daddy Derek say.

For a little girl, I made pretty good grades in school. But I had more than book smarts. Mom and Dad always told me that I was blessed with common sense. Before he left, Dad taught me things because he wanted me to be able to take care of myself. After my parents got a divorce, Mom took good care of me all by herself. She taught me that everything was going to be okay.

Then I had to be a big girl and accept that my dad was going off far away to serve our country. Although he'd been okay so far off the coast of Africa on his naval ship, the news now seemed to be different.

I couldn't take it any longer. I burst into their bedroom and said, "My dad's ship is in trouble?"

My mom stood up and rushed to me. Wrapping her

arms around me, she said, "We don't know that for sure, baby. We're going to hold on to hope and faith. We have to pray and believe that he's okay."

"But look at the TV!" I said, pointing to the big screen that was high up on the wall.

They couldn't hide any news from me with the pictures they were showing on the screen. If my dad was in trouble, no one could make the worst thing in the world go away. I knew something bad was happening but I needed to hear it from them.

"Tell me, Mom. Daddy Derek. Tell me, please!"

Daddy Derek held out his arms and I went to him. He hugged me tight. I knew from his heart beating so loudly that he was worried too. He prayed, "Lord, I ask You to keep Officer Monty Love safe. We don't know what's going on. Please don't let anyone be hurt. The news said a ship in his area was attacked. Lord, we know that You care and You love us, so we pray that it's not his ship. You give us the strength to trust in Your plan. Help little Morgan with whatever is Your will. In Jesus' name, we pray. Amen."

"Okay," I said, wiping tears from my eyes. I was going to be a big girl about this. Wanting to hear from my dad, I told them, "We gotta call him."

Mom said, "I already tried to call him, but we're not able to get through right now. I'm trying, baby."

"We need to try harder. We gotta get on the computer. We need to find him," I said, pulling at her robe for her to move and do more.

She went to a drawer and pulled out some papers that had information about where my dad was. Mom started calling the office numbers, but no one had the answers. Daddy Derek took the phone to take over the **exchange** while Mom talked to me.

"Everything is going to be okay, baby. God is watching over your daddy," she whispered in my ear.

I pulled away. "How do we know everything will be okay when we don't even know what's wrong?"

She took my hand and led me into the kitchen. She didn't even know that I got up in the first place to get some warm milk, but she opened the refrigerator and pulled out the bottle. Then she reached into the cabinet to grab me a cup and poured me some. I'm not sure if she realized which cup she picked, but it read, "Daddy's Girl."

After she heated the cup in the microwave oven, I drank a little and tears fell into my cup. I tried so hard to hold it together, but the tears kept falling worse than Jack and Jill rolling down the hill. When I couldn't hold on any longer, I dropped my mug on the floor.

"Oh, my goodness! I broke my mug that Daddy gave me! He's gone, Mom! That means he's gone!"

"Morgan! No, sweetie. You can't do that, baby. You have to know that Jesus is with your dad. Just hold on to that thought. Okay?"

As soon as she said that, it made me feel a lot better. So I tried hard to get a **grip** on myself and pull it together. I was going to fight my doubts and stay positive.

While Mom cleaned up the mess, I said, "Thank you, Mom. It really is gonna be okay. We have to have faith that God will handle it for us."

"Yes, baby, that's right. The Word of God says that if you have faith the size of a mustard seed, that's enough faith for God to make the impossible to happen."

Mama and Papa told me to remember Psalm 23 whenever I was afraid, so I started saying it in my mind. The words reminded me that we don't ever have to be afraid because God is always with us.

"He's okay!" Daddy Derek said, running into the kitchen and shouting joyfully. "It wasn't his ship. I spoke to a Navy officer and they're going to contact all of the families tomorrow and give them the news!"

I ran right to Mom as soon as I heard the good report. I was going to see Daddy again! It was such a good feeling. I jumped from my mom to Daddy Derek, saying, "Thank you! Thank you!"

"I wanted him to be okay too, pumpkin. Now, we have to continue to pray for his safety and the families who were harmed by that **brutal** attack. It's great to know that the Lord answered our prayers. I'm glad you can be happy now that we know it wasn't his ship. Thinking that he might have been hurt was a scary thought."

Letter to Dad

Dear Dad,

I love you so much. I am happy to report that I'm in tutoring so I can excel. A girl in my class named Greta is rough around the edges. At least, that's the way Mama puts it. That means Greta is not that refined. She told me I thought I was too good for tutoring.

At first I was devastated, but I learned she just wanted us to be friends. Oh yeah, Dad, also I got a subpoena. Mom says I have to exchange information with the clerk or maybe I have to testify and give information. I don't want to, but Mom says she'll be with me.

The biggest thing that happened was when I had to get a grip on my thoughts because I thought I'd lost you. I heard about the other navy ship that was in the brutal attack. I'm so sad for those families, but I'm proud of those men who fight for our country. Most of all, I'm glad God kept you safe, Dad.

Your daughter,

Daddy's girl, Morgan

Word Search

```
Q  C  Y  K  S  E  F  F  E  C  T  S
U  A  O  N  U  R  B  O  L  L  D  Q
I  U  E  I  B  B  G  E  A  E  E  U
E  S  G  C  P  O  C  H  T  A  N  E
T  E  N  K  O  X  I  A  B  R  I  S
L  S  A  E  E  F  T  J  R  N  F  T
Y  X  H  R  N  S  Y  G  O  I  E  I
T  A  C  S  A  L  K  R  O  N  R  O
R  N  X  V  L  P  C  I  K  G  B  N
E  D  E  I  S  N  A  P  E  W  Z  S
Y  D  B  D  M  B  R  U  T  A  L  T
A  N  S  W  E  R  I  N  G  O  N  E
```

BRUTAL

DEVASTATED

EXCEL

EXCHANGE

GRIP

REFINED

SUBPOENA

Words to Know and Learn

1) **ex·cel** (ĭk-sĕl') *verb*
To do or be better than; surpass.

2) **re·fined** (rĭ-fīnd') *adjective*
Showing qualities of sensitivity or taste.

3) **dev·as·tat·e** (dĕv'ə-stāt') *verb* **dev·as·tat·ed** (past tense)
To feel overwhelmed or stunned; be greatly upset.

4) **sub·poe·na** (sə-pē'nə) *noun*
A written order requiring appearance in court to give testimony.

5) **ex·change** (ĭks-chānj') *verb*
To give in return for something received; trade; to give up for a substitute.

6) **grip** (grĭp) *noun*
A tight hold; a firm grasp.

7) **bru·tal** (brūt'l) *adjective*
Extremely ruthless or cruel; harsh.

Chapter 4

Bad News

On the playground, I watched as everybody around me participated in the fun. But it was too hard for me to enjoy myself. I wasn't ready for this test that was coming faster than the sparrow that just flew by. I really didn't want to be a witness against Bridget even though she came into the washroom with her friends and stole my iPod.

But, it wasn't right for me to worry about any of that. When I thought about what Jesus would do, worrying is not the answer.

Of course, I was supposed to have faith and believe Jesus had the answers. But since I'm a kid, **implementing** the idea of trusting Him wasn't always so easy. It was just hard for me to have fun when I was upset about all this stuff.

Looking across the playground, I was very happy to see

Tim dancing around everyone, smiling and playing. He was such a good kid and we all had gotten used to him. Tim was our buddy and he'd gotten used to us too. Although some people may think he's not perfect, well my answer to that is, nobody's perfect.

But Tim was perfectly tuned in to us. He saw me and started dancing over to me. "Come on, friend Morgan. Play."

"I'm all right, Tim. I'm watchin' you."

"Ooh, ooh. Watch me kick! Watch me kick!" he said.

Tim hopped away to play kickball. I looked around the playground and saw Billy standing by himself under a tree. He was looking at me real hard and frowning. His expression was so scary that it could almost be a Halloween mask. When he saw my eyes meet his, he made his frown worse. Right away, I frowned back.

When Billy saw me not taking my eyes off of him, he came over and shoved me. "You make me sick. I can't believe you!" he yelled.

I just stood there and dropped my hands. I gave him a confused look like, *What are you talking about?*

"No fight. No fightin' friend Morgan," Tim said, as he pulled Billy away from me.

Billy tugged away from Tim saying, "Let go of my arm!"

Just then Alec saw what was going on and said to Billy, "I know you're not tryin' to fight Tim."

"Stay out of this, Alec. I don't have a problem with Tim or you. *She's* my problem," he said, pointing at me as if I'd stolen something from his sister instead of the other way around. He started toward me again.

"No, man. I'm not gonna let you fight a girl."

"No, man. No hurt friend Morgan," Tim said, balling up his fists.

"I know Morgan didn't do one thing to you. Why are you trippin'?" Alec asked, trying to push Tim back. But Tim wouldn't leave me because he felt I was in danger.

Brooke came over to me and grabbed my arm. Greta came running over too, acting all excited.

"Oh, my goodness! Are you hurt? Do you need me to get the nurse or Mrs. Hardy? Mrs. Hardy, help!" Greta called out, before Brooke took her hand and covered Greta's big mouth.

Frowning at Greta, she said, "Shhhh! No one wants to go in early from recess. Be quiet and we'll figure this out."

I said, "Thanks, Greta, but it's cool."

She took Brooke's hand off her face. "What, you don't wanna talk to me? You don't want me to help you?"

I didn't know what to say. I wasn't trying to make Greta feel like I didn't want to talk to her. At the same time, Billy wasn't moving away from me. I didn't want all of that attention on me, so I just turned my back and walked away.

"Come back here! This isn't over," Billy called out.

Brooke rushed by my side and Greta to the other. "What's going on with him?" Brooke asked me. "What did you do to him?"

I shrugged and said, "I don't know. I didn't do any-thing. He was just staring at me and I stared back. He got this attitude and started rollin' his eyes at me, lookin' at me like he wanted to fight."

"For Billy to get upset, you must have done somethin' bad. Billy doesn't usually fight girls. But he does have a big sister, so he's probably not scared to hit a girl."

"You come back here, Morgan," Billy said.

I just turned around. "You know what, I'm not gonna run from him. If he has somethin' to say to me, then we need to deal with it."

I walked right up to his face. "What did I do to you, Billy?" I asked him.

"It's not what you did to me. It's what you did to my sister. You're gonna be a witness against her in court and put her in jail. I can't stand you." His eyes looked like fire.

All of my friends just looked at me in surprise. I couldn't even face them. I could feel coldness around me and it wasn't coming from the 65-degree weather we were having in March. I just needed to go home and get under my covers.

"Is this true?" Alec asked me. I could tell he was hoping it wasn't.

"Alec, don't say it like I *wanna* testify against his sister," I said, tired of them thinking I was the bad one. "Listen up, everybody, I got a subpoena. I didn't even know what that was. I'm very worried about it and haven't been able to sleep. My mom is trying really hard to get me out of it. So I hope I won't even have to go."

Then I turned to Billy and said, "You know me better than that. Your sister stole from me and I'm just doing what I have to do, not what I wanna do. I forgave her and dropped it. I didn't wanna make her life worse. But even my grandparents told me when you do the wrong thing, there are consequences. And this isn't even her first time."

My friends were listening and nodding like they understood. I kept talking to Billy. "When I had to go to the hospital and get stitches, I didn't hear you apologize once for what she did to me."

"My family is goin' through a lot," Billy said, as his chubby caramel-colored face turned red like a candy apple.

"And so is mine. My dad is far away serving our country on a ship somewhere. I'm worried sick about passing the big test that we all have to take next month. I'm not tryin' to hurt anybody, and I don't want anyone to try and hurt me."

"Yeah, Billy," said Alec.

"Yeah, Billy," said Tim.

"Yeah, Billy," Brooke and Greta said together.

"Yeah, Billy," everybody in our class joined in. That's when I saw we had a big crowd.

Before he spoke, Billy shook his head and thought over what I told him.

"I'm sorry, Morgan. I guess messin' with you was the only thing I could do."

I'm glad he knew that I wasn't trying to hurt his family

intentionally. I'm glad he came to his senses, because I wasn't going to fight him.

• • • • •

It was Wednesday night and Daddy Derek was leading children's Bible study. "Today, we're going to read from the book of Esther. It's an Old Testament book about faith, courage, and devotion to God. Esther's story is really important because she was brave and she was able to save her people. This story shows that God has a plan for our lives, and He's always working for the good of His people. I think it's great that women can be strong and **dynamic** too."

If I ever needed to hear about how to be brave, now was the time. Fear was trying to take over my mind. I just looked up to heaven and prayed, *Lord, I thank You for allowing me to come to church. I hope I learn something that brings me closer to You. Let Your Word keep me from being so scared.*

Daddy Derek began reading the story. "King Xerxes ruled over the land of Persia, and it was a mighty land. He wanted a wife, and his servants brought many women to the palace so that the king could choose his bride. After about a year, he chose a young lady by the name of Esther. She was good, smart, and very pretty. She was also Jewish, one of the children of Israel. If the king found out, that could cause a problem for him."

Everyone looked at each other and couldn't figure out

what could be wrong with that. Daddy Derek was playing with us and wouldn't go on with the story because we wanted to know!

"I guess you guys want me to keep going?" he teased.

"Yes, read!" someone shouted.

"A man named Mordecai adopted Esther. He was actually her cousin but he raised her as his own child. However, he told her not to tell anyone that she was one of the children of Israel."

Again, we looked around like, *Why did that need to be a secret?*

Daddy Derek continued, "Well, at that time, many people didn't think it was good to be Jewish. But when King Xerxes saw Esther, he really liked her. He put a crown on her head and she became his wife. Now Esther was the queen of Persia. There was a big celebration for the new queen. Her cousin Mordecai often sat by the palace gates, just so he'd know how Esther was doing. One time he heard some mean men saying that they were going to kill the king. Mordecai went to tell Esther and Esther told the king. The bad men were arrested and Mordecai's good deed and effort was written down in the king's record book."

"It was good that Mordecai was there, huh?" a boy in our group said.

"It was very good that he was there. Later on, a really powerful man named Haman became angry at Mordecai. Haman found out that Mordecai was Jewish and he encouraged King Xerxes to make it legal to kill all of Esther's people. King Xerxes agreed. Esther got scared when she found out because she knew she would die too. But the king didn't know that Esther was a Jew. Though Esther was scared, she told Mordecai that she would do everything she could to change the situation. Since she knew it meant that she might be killed, she told her cousin to ask all of the Jewish people to pray for her."

I was sitting there listening and I was thinking, *Wow. Even though Esther was scared because she knew that she could die, she was still strong. I think that was real brave of her.*

Daddy Derek kept going, "Esther wanted to speak to her husband, the king. She came close to him and he asked what he could do for her. He told her he would give her whatever she wanted, even half of his kingdom."

"Wow," the same boy said. "He was gonna give her his kingdom? I'd never do that if I was him."

"You never know what love will have you do," Daddy Derek said and smiled. He continued with his story. "Esther told the king she was planning a big supper for him and Haman. Again, the king was so pleased that he asked Esther what he could give her. She told him to come to the banquet tomorrow and she would tell him. She knew the king would do what she wanted. So, at the banquet, Esther asked him to spare her life and the lives of her people. She told him it wasn't fair and they didn't deserve to die. When the king asked Esther, 'How is this so?,' Esther pointed to

Haman because he was behind it all. The king didn't like that and he ordered Haman to be killed."

Daddy Derek looked around the room. He could tell we were paying attention and we all enjoyed the story very much. So he finished by saying, "Esther had saved her people. She put her life on the line and prayed. God showed her that when we trust Him, everything will turn out for our good. So whenever something is troubling you, young people, take that fear to God. Don't let your fears have power over you. Give your problems to God and trust Him to work them out."

I put my hands together and thanked God. I wanted to be like Esther. I wanted to be brave. I really didn't want to be afraid. I wanted to put my faith in God so that I would have no fear. Now God had given me a great story to think on that would help me do just that.

I went up to Daddy Derek and hugged him. "Thank you. I needed that."

"I know," he said.

A few seconds later, Mom walked into our meeting and told Daddy Derek, "We're not going to be able to leave yet. Hold the children. It's raining pretty hard out there."

The next thing we knew, the storm blew out the power and the lights went out. So we had snacks and sang songs of praise. It was all good. We could ride out the storm and I wasn't even scared of the lightning and thunder. I guess the story of Esther was working. Yay!

●　●　●　●　●

On the way to school Thursday morning, the bus driver had to be extra careful because the storm had left twigs and branches all over the street. As I looked around, I thought about last night and was really glad when the storm had ended. At school, everyone was talking about how afraid they were. Even at church we had to stop singing, sit in the corner, and quiet down. It was pretty scary when some hail hit the window and shattered the glass.

"My family had to go down to the basement so we could **barricade** ourselves," Trey said, remembering the stormy night.

"I slept with my mom," Brooke said, hugging herself.

"My brother Antoine tried to act like he wasn't scared," Alec joined in. "But he was scared. When a tree fell up against our house, both of us ran to our parents' room." Then he said something that sounded kind of funny. "I'm glad the storm happened."

"If a tree fell on your house and you were scared, what were you glad about?" Brooke asked, as the rest of us listened for his answer.

He smiled. "My parents were arguing before the storm and then it kind of brought them together."

I just nodded my head, thinking I'd "been there and done that." Then I told them my story from church and what I learned about Esther. It was cool to share it with them. Billy tried to act like he didn't like my story, but I knew he was listening. Even boys could learn from Esther's story. She taught us to stand strong even when we were afraid.

"Okay, class, enough of the **chitchat**. It's time to get to work. Remember, the CRCT is just four weeks away," said Mrs. Hardy.

She passed out some new worksheets and we all got busy. I was ready to take my practice tests before the big one. It was really quiet in the room while we were doing our work. No one said a word. Then Alec, Trey, Brooke, and I looked up at the same time.

Billy asked, "Where's Tim?"

"I was thinking the same thing," said Alec.

Brooke said, "Me too. It's too quiet in here."

"Yeah. My boy isn't here to lighten things up," said Trey.

Mrs. Hardy didn't answer. She got our attention by saying, "Class, let's go over rounding to the nearest ten thousandth. For our first example, if you have the number 15,607, you don't look in the ones, tens, or hundreds place. You look at the number that is in the thousands place. In this case, it is a 5. If the number is 5 or more you round up to 20,000.

"If you have the number 67,052, you don't look in the ones, tens, or hundreds place but you look at the 7. Since it's more than 5 then you round up to 70,000. If you have the number 31,979, you don't look in the ones, tens, or hundreds place but you look at the 1. Since it's lower than 5, you keep it at 30,000. Understood?"

We all nodded our heads and she told us to work the problems. I finished my math worksheet first and turned it in. I raised my hand to ask Mrs. Hardy if it was okay to go to the washroom. She said it was okay and I got up quietly to leave the room.

Just before I stepped out, the school secretary came over the intercom and asked if Mrs. Hardy could come to the office. Dr. Sharpe wanted to see her, so Mrs. Hardy and I walked out together.

When I turned to go to the washroom, there was a lot of **commotion** going on around the principal's office. I saw Tim's mother and remembered how nice she had spoken to me when I got in trouble for making fun of him. She was crying and I wondered what had happened. Some other people were waiting at the office door for Mrs. Hardy to come too. I didn't know what was going on, but when I heard Mrs. Hardy cry out from all the way in the washroom, I got scared.

I rushed back to our classroom. "Oh, my goodness, you guys. Something isn't right with Mrs. Hardy."

"What do you mean?" Alec asked.

Just then we saw car lights flash across the window. Brooke rushed over to look out and said, "There's a police car out there."

"Must be somethin' goin' on with her family," said Billy.

"It can't be anything with her family. She's been too happy," I said.

"Yeah, but they might be comin' to tell her some bad

news. It happens to me all the time. Life is pretty good and then all of a sudden, I get the news that makes everything bad," Billy said.

"Morgan," Alec called out my name. He was looking out the window into the parking lot. "Your mom is pulling up to the school."

I rushed over to the window. Alec and Brooke were both right. Mom was here. Also, parents and police were everywhere.

Then Alec had to take another look, saying, "Huh? My dad is too. What's going on?"

Trey came and looked out. "And there's my mom! The last time all of our parents came to school we were getting a talk about school violence."

I tried not to get scared. I didn't wanna guess about what was going on. None of us knew. So I **exhaled** and said, "Y'all, I want to pray."

Alec said, "Pray for all of us."

I bowed my head and said, "Lord, we don't know what's going on, but please help us. In Jesus' name, I pray. Amen."

Not much longer after I prayed, Mrs. Hardy walked in with a tissue in her hand. Right behind her was Dr. Sharpe and the school's resource officer. Our parents came in after them. We didn't know what our parents were doing at school in the middle of the day. My mom walked right over to me and held my hand.

"Mom, what's goin' on?" I asked her.

"Everything is going to be okay, sweetheart," she said, as she kissed my forehead.

A stranger walked to the front of our class and said, "Hi, I'm Dr. Morris. I'm here from the school system. We want you to stay calm, but we must talk to you about your classmate, Tim."

"Where is he?" Trey called out. Trey's mom just burst out crying.

"We have some very bad news."

Letter to Dad

Dear Dad,

I'm having a hard time implementing my faith in God. Dad, now I know why Mama always says "if it ain't one thing it's another." See, I never have a break. Intentionally, I want to have an easy life because I'm a kid. I'm not dynamic, but I think I'm an okay person. So then, why is it always drama?

My friend Billy tried to fight me on the playground. He told everyone that I was trying to hurt his sister. But all my other friends formed a barricade around me. Well, I had a little chitchat with him and let him know I don't want to be a witness against her. After all of the commotion, he exhaled and realized I was cool.

Now we found out some news about our friend Tim. Told you it's always something.

Your daughter,
Frustrated Morgan

Word Search

I B S H A R P E N Z B X
M A X J C H I T C H A T
P R A Q D A P B O S R M
L C T D R R E A M C R O
E O W E A D R R M H I R
M D A L M Y R N O O C G
E E T A A N Y E T O A A
N B E H T R E Y I L D N
T O R X L A M O O R E D
I N T E N T I O N A L N
N P A U L D Y N A M I C
G S T E P H A N I E Z F

BARRICADE

CHITCHAT

COMMOTION

DYNAMIC

EXHALED

IMPLEMENTING

INTENTIONAL

Words to Know and Learn

1) **im·ple·ment** (ĭm'plə-mənt) *verb*
To put into effect; carry out.

2) **in·ten·tion·al** (ĭn-tĕn'shə-nəl) *adjective*
in·tention·al·ly *adverb*
Done deliberately.

3) **dy·nam·ic** (dī-năm'ĭk) *adjective*
Marked by energy and strength; forceful.

4) **bar·ri·cade** (băr'ĭ-kād', băr'ĭ-kād') *noun*
Something that serves as an obstacle; a barrier.

5) **chit·chat** (chĭt-chăt) *noun*
Casual conversation; small talk.

6) **com·mo·tion** (kə-mō'shən) *noun*
A disturbance; disorder.

7) **ex·hale** (ĕks-hāl', ĕk-sāl') *verb*
ex·haled past tense
To breathe out.

Chapter 5

Forever Thankful

"Tim and his father were in a really bad car accident last night," Dr. Morris said to us.

"Oh, no! What hospital are they in? Can we all go and visit them? We'll take Tim a get-well card," I said. Then my mom hugged me really tight to keep me quiet.

"Dear, let me explain."

"Yes, sweetheart, let him finish, Morgan," Mom said, rubbing my cheek.

"But we can go and make him feel better. He'll be okay if he sees us coming to cheer him up," I looked up and told her.

"Yeah. Morgan came to see me and that lit up my whole day," Billy called out.

The man who was speaking to us turned around to Mrs. Hardy and said, "This is going to be harder than I thought."

"Children, I really need you to listen. Please let the

gentleman finish and we'll take your questions at the end," Mrs. Hardy said to us.

I did as Mrs. Hardy asked. But something told me that this wasn't good news at all. Dr. Morris already said it was bad news, but it seemed like it was worse than bad news. I don't think I was ready for more bad news. I wished these events were not **occurring** right now. Mom could feel my pain. She grabbed my hand again and squeezed it tight.

Dr. Morris continued, "The storm was quite severe last night. Tim and his father both were **tragically** killed in a car crash."

After that, all I heard were yells, screaming, crying, and shouting. Alec put his head down on his desk. All I could do was sit there. I couldn't move. Did Dr. Morris really just say that happened?

"Morgan, are you all right. Talk me to, honey. Did you hear what the man just said?" Mom was shaking me lightly to get me to move.

"I can't believe this, Mom!" I finally shouted. "I just finished praying before all of you came in here. I prayed for everything to be okay. How could this happen?"

"It's all right, Morgan. Tim is with the Lord," Mom said, as she put her hand over her heart.

"How do you know he's with the Lord?" I asked.

"When we were in the office this morning, Tim's mom told us that Tim is a believer."

"Oh, Mom," I said, feeling as bad as I did when I thought my dad was gone.

Dr. Morris spoke up. "I know this is a lot for you all to handle right now. You were close to him and he was your friend. With your tests coming up soon, know that the school is here to help you manage any stress that you may have."

This just didn't seem right or fair. Tim was so young. I just didn't get it. What were we supposed to do or say?

"It's fine with me. I didn't like him anyway," Billy said even though his eyes were watery.

Trey went over and punched him in the arm. "Stop tellin' a fib. You're just sayin' that so you won't have to feel like we feel. You were lookin' for him this morning just like the rest of us."

Brooke started crying real loud. She kept saying this hurt so badly. Greta was crying too. Then Trey started crying. When tough Alec started crying, I didn't know how we were gonna deal with this terrible news.

Dr. Sharpe added, "At first we were looking for the best class to place Tim in. He was ready to be in a regular class and you guys welcomed him. I used to see him in the hallways, happy and playful. Though his life was difficult and he had different needs, he felt truly special because of you. It's clear that he made an **impact** on you too. You should be proud because you knew him. Now, your parents will take you home, but Dr. Morris and a few other people are here if you want to stay and talk. This will be hard for all of us to deal with, but in time we will get through it. We will find the strength to be okay."

I held back my tears and silently prayed, *Lord, help us*

all deal with this big loss. Amen.

• • • • •

Most of the kids in my class wanted to stay together. My mom saw that I was too shaken up. So she told them she was going to take me home and I'd see my friends later. I gathered up my books and things and headed to the classroom door.

Brooke came over to me and said, "Morgan, I'm glad we're friends."

"I'm glad too," I said to her, as we gave each other a huge hug.

"I just wanted to say that because you never know what could happen." We hugged again.

She was right, though. Sometimes bad things just happen. But the more I thought about Tim, I became afraid to die. It was getting harder to stop thinking about it.

When we got in the car, I wasn't saying a word, but Mom did. "Morgan, I know this is a lot for you and you're very upset, but this is not completely a bad thing."

"What do you mean, Mom? My friend is gone!" I said angrily. "You should have seen him yesterday and on the playground last week. He was so happy. This is just really bad news."

"I told you he's with God, sweetie. Yes, you're going to miss your friend. It's bad that his mom is going to miss her little boy, but it's a good thing that he's in the arms of Jesus. Right?"

I just sat there, thinking about what she just told me. She was my mom and I wasn't trying to talk back. I was pretty much expected to say yes ma'am to everything she said. My lips couldn't even move to speak. I nodded my head and stared out the window all the way home.

Mama, Papa, Daddy Derek, and little Jayden were all waiting when we got home. They were ready to wrap their arms around me. With each hug, I could tell that they really cared and didn't want me to be sad. But their wish didn't work because I was feeling really bad.

"Can I go to sleep, Mom?" I said in my saddest voice.

"You need to eat something first, Morgan."

She made me a ham sandwich, with a pickle on the side and some chips. Although it was one of my favorite meals, right then I just couldn't eat. Papa looked at me and I looked down at my plate.

"I know how you feel, baby. Lately, I've been losing some of my friends too and it doesn't feel good . . ."

As Papa kept talking, I was getting angrier by the minute. Finally, I spoke up and said, "I'm sorry, Papa. But my friend was only eight years old. It's not the same. Mom, I don't want anything to eat."

"Okay, baby. Go to bed."

I wasn't trying to hurt anyone's feelings. They were just trying to help me. Maybe I just needed to be alone for a while. When I reached my room, I dropped to my knees and folded my hands tight.

"Lord, this hurts. This hurts bad. That's all I have to say."

I got up off the floor, kicked off my shoes, kept on my clothes, and snuggled up tight under the covers. Closing my eyes, I tried to sleep. But all of a sudden, I was having a bad dream and felt like I couldn't breathe. I didn't know if it was about Tim or about me, but I was **petrified**.

I screamed out and all of the adults came rushing in. "Morgan, what is it?" Mom said.

"Oh, my goodness. Look at that child. She's sweating," Mama said, feeling my forehead.

"I don't wanna die! I don't wanna die! It's scary. Help me!" I screamed.

Daddy Derek sat on the other side of me and said, "No, it's not, sweetheart. You don't have to be afraid. Tim doesn't hear, see, or feel anything like you can right now. He's not scared. Heaven is a place we haven't seen or can even imagine. But God is there and it's all good. You just think about all your favorite places to go and your favorite things to do, and know that heaven is ten times better than that."

"I just don't understand why it has to be like this. I don't understand why it happened."

Daddy Derek said, "Morgan, the Lord will teach you how to trust Him, if you ask Him to. One day when we go to heaven, He might take us aside and He might explain the stuff we don't understand. Until then, we have to be here on earth and be thankful."

I was trying hard to understand what he was saying, but my feelings were all over the place. Daddy Derek could see from the look on my face that he had some more explaining to do, so he continued. "You see, Morgan, it's not just about the grave. You know the story of Easter and Jesus dying on the cross. He got back up from the grave. He paid that tough price so that Tim could have the life he has now with Jesus."

Then, I started feeling better when Daddy Derek told me, "Tim is happy. He's living it up. That's why you don't need to be afraid. God loves each one of us so much that He sent His only Son to die for us. He wants us to have a life that goes on forever. That's the greatest thing there is, baby."

Thinking about what it must be like to be with God, I nodded and the pain in my heart stopped hurting so bad. I felt so much better.

• • • • •

As if I didn't have a tough enough day when I heard about Tim, the next day wasn't getting any better. Not only did I have to go to school today, but I had to go to court first.

"Come on, Morgan, we're going to be late," Mom yelled out. "This is my third time calling you, let's go!"

I was dragging my feet. I didn't want to go sit in a big chair and raise my hand to tell the truth. I didn't want to send Billy's sister, Bridget, to jail or wherever they send kids. All I could think about was when Bridget got out and I'd be the first one she'd come to for **retaliation**.

When we were in the car, Mom said, "Morgan, I

understand this is not something that you want to do. Trust me, I don't want you to do it either. I tried to help you understand that life isn't going to be easy and sometimes things are out of your control. The best thing you can do is to get this over with and move on. Everybody has issues. You have to learn not to pout and just face up to painful situations. Deal with it the best way you can, sweetie."

It had been a long time since Mom gave me some tough-love talk like that. I understood what she said and knew she was right. Still I was scared and I didn't want to go to court. But what was having a sour attitude going to do about my situation? Really nothing but make it worse.

I had already learned that when you have a good attitude, things won't be as bad. Now I just needed to apply the things I already knew. So I told myself, *Okay. Now, I'm ready!*

But then we arrived about the same time as Bridget, her mother, and Miss May.

"Hey, y'all," Miss May called out.

We stopped so they could catch up with us. Mom and the two ladies started talking. As soon as Mom turned her back to open the door, Bridget bumped into me. She didn't say anything, but she didn't need to. All of my hopes of us still getting along went right out the window. That's the message I got, without her even saying that she was gonna get me.

We walked into the building. First, the ladies had to put their purses through a machine to make sure no one had any weapons. Police officers were standing close by to make sure everyone followed the law. An officer told Mom and me to go one way and Miss May, Bridget, and her mother were told to go another way.

Feeling afraid again, I said, "Mom, I don't wanna do this."

All of a sudden, she must have gotten a bright idea because she told me, "Hold on." I didn't know what she was about to do, but Mom was looking at a clerk sitting at a desk. I could tell something was on her mind.

"Sit right here and I'll be back."

She went over to talk to the man at the desk. I wasn't sure what she was saying, but I hoped she was getting me out of this mess. I sure didn't want to be there. Then I got a happy feeling about whatever she had said, as I watched her come back.

"Okay, sweetie. Let's go."

I perked up right away. "You mean, we can leave? I don't have to sit up there in that big box next to the judge and tell the truth?"

"Girl, I said come on," she said, laughing at the fact that I was so excited we could go.

I was ecstatic. I was thrilled. I didn't have to say anything that would make Bridget wanna beat me up later on. Mom told me to come on and she didn't have to tell me twice. We walked right out the door.

"Thanks, Mom!" I said, hugging her. "How did you do it, Mom? What did you say to make me not have to say anything?"

"I just told them, as a parent, I didn't want you to testify. I felt like you didn't have to say anything. Since they already saw Bridget on videotape, it didn't matter whether she told the truth or not because they had enough evidence."

"I just feel so bad for her, Mom. What will happen to her?"

"The clerk said the judge will most likely give her **probation**."

"What's that?"

"That means if she does another bad thing like stealing from someone, she will have to go to a jail for young people. Hopefully, that won't happen. Now let's go and get some breakfast before I take you to school."

"Okay!"

I could tell Mom wanted to talk to me and have a big-girl conversation. Time together with her meant a lot to me. I waited and waited until I had my waffles, scrambled eggs with cheese, two strips of bacon, and a tall glass of orange juice. Then I just couldn't take it anymore.

"Mom! Talk to me."

"I know, baby. I'm just sorry that you're going through so much. I want to protect you, but there's only so much that I can keep from you. You're going to live your own life and make your own choices. I just have to trust that you'll do the right thing."

I reached over and grabbed her hand and said, "Mom, I know you worry about me, but you're doing a good job of raising me. Mama, Papa, and Daddy Derek are always there to keep me straight too. And I know Dad is on his ship praying for me. I'm gonna be okay because I believe in God. I wanna accept Christ into my heart. If today is my last day, I want you to know that I'm going to be in heaven. Can you help me do that?"

Mom's eyes watered up almost as full as the water in her glass. "I guess I have been doing a good job with you, Miss Morgan. If that's a desire in your heart, let's pray the prayer of **salvation**. You just tell God what you just told me and He'll hear you."

My parents have been taking me to church ever since I was a little girl. And I've heard ministers talk about the prayer of salvation. Remembering what they've said, I prayed aloud, "Lord, in John 3:16, it says You so loved the world that You gave Your only begotten Son and that whoever believes in Him shall not perish but have everlasting life. I know that You love me and I accept You into my heart. You will be in my heart always. Amen."

Then I squeezed my mom's hand, and she prayed, "Lord, I thank You for my daughter, Morgan. I am so happy that You knocked on the door of her heart and she opened the door to let You in. I know that she is dealing with a lot as a little girl, but I also know that You won't give her more than she can handle. Thank You for being with her always. Thank You for sending Your only Son to die on the cross and take away our sins. You have blessed us and we will be forever thankful."

Letter to Dad

Dear Dad,

Well, a lot of bad things are occurring in my life. Tragically, my friend Tim died in a car crash. The impact the car took was too much. At first I was petrified about dying after Tim died. But Daddy Derek helped me to understand Jesus beat the grave and heaven is better than I can imagine.

Also, I had to go to court and the girl who took my iPod thought I showed up in retaliation. Mom worked it out so I didn't have to testify, though, and Bridget got probation.

Best of all, I accepted Jesus Christ into my heart! Now my salvation is secure.

Your daughter,
Saved Morgan

Word Search

```
W  A  Y  L  L  A  C  I  G  A  R  T
P  C  G  B  E  A  N  S  R  S  E  S
P  C  P  N  T  R  A  G  I  C  T  A
E  I  O  A  I  N  J  T  C  T  A  L
T  D  P  T  M  R  P  R  E  O  L  V
R  E  C  I  P  M  R  O  K  L  I  A
I  N  O  O  A  B  Y  U  Q  L  A  T
F  D  R  N  C  O  M  R  C  R  T  I
I  S  N  T  T  X  V  L  R  C  I  O
E  F  R  A  N  K  S  E  T  H  O  N
D  X  P  R  O  B  A  T  I  O  N  C
C  A  R  N  A  T  I  O  N  Z  E  H
```

IMPACT

OCCURRING

PETRIFIED

PROBATION

RETALIATION

SALVATION

TRAGICALLY

Words to Know and Learn

1) **oc·cur** (ə-kûr') *verb*
oc·cur·ring
To take place; come about; happen.

2) **trag·ic** (trăj'ĭk) *adjective* **trag·ic·cal·ly** *adverb*
Having to do with death, disaster, or destruction.

3) **im·pact** (ĭm'păkt') *noun*
The effect or impression of one thing on another; or a collision.

4) **pet·ri·fy** (pĕt'rə-fī') *verb* **pet·ri·fied** (past tense)
To stun or paralyze with terror; daze.

5) **re·tal·i·ate** (rĭ-tăl'ē-āt') *verb* **re·tal·i·a·tion** *noun*
To return like for like, especially evil for evil.

6) **pro·ba·tion** (prō-bā'shən) *noun*
Allowing a person who have been convicted of an offense to not go to jail,
but to remain free provided he or she stays out of trouble.

7) **sal·va·tion** (săl-vā'shən) *noun*
In the religious sense: deliverance from evil and its eternal consequences.

Chapter 6

Fly Away

Without Tim, the next couple of days in school were really hard. When I looked at the desk he sat in, no one was there. The things he said to make us laugh, now no one was saying. The bright smiles he gave, we saw on no one's face. Tim left an empty space in all of our hearts and I really didn't know if I'd be the same again.

I particularly didn't want to go to tutoring. Not because I didn't want to learn all I could for the standard test, but it wasn't the same without Tim being there. When I got a wrong answer and didn't think I could do any better, Tim always said something to give me hope. I just stared at the blank computer screen, not even wanting to turn it on. In my mind, I was thinking about everything but the test.

Then, I heard Greta say, "Morgan, I'm scared."

I wanted to say, "me too." But I took a deep breath and

thought about Esther. I knew at this time I needed to be there for my classmates.

"What are you afraid of?" I asked.

She opened up and said, "I'm afraid I won't ever have any friends. I'm worried that I'll never be as well liked as Tim was. I always say the wrong things and no one wants to hang out with me. I think I'm gonna always be alone. I want people to care about me like they cared about Tim or about you. I just don't know how to change things."

I wanted to tell Greta to quit making things sound so bad, but I couldn't say anything because she was exactly right. Most of the time she found a way to upset things, but now she was in a different place. I remember last summer when I had to deal with my self-esteem. So I asked her, "Are you happy with yourself?"

She looked up at the ceiling and thought about my question. I didn't want to rush her because that question was very important. And I know it can be hard to answer. After all, if you don't like yourself, how could anybody else like you?

She said, "No."

Tears started to fall slowly from her eyes, like on a cloudy, rainy day. Quickly, I got up and went over to the tutor's desk and grabbed some pieces of tissue, one after another. I handed them to Greta and patted her back.

"It's okay, Greta," I told her.

"I want people to like me, Morgan, but it's not that easy for me. I say the wrong things and run people away. I wouldn't wanna listen to **sarcastic** people all day either. Who wants a friend like that? But you don't know what I'm talkin' about or what I'm goin' through. I don't know why I asked you to help me."

"You asked me because you want us to be friends. If you give me a chance to tell you my story, you'll see I'm just like you. Most of last year, I was by myself and no one wanted to be my friend. I was on the **outskirts**. My mom used to tell me that I could handle having no friends and I was fine being alone. But it bothered me a lot anyway. Sometimes people got mad at me for stuff that was dumb. Also, I had to keep checking myself and found out that I was jealous of my friends. I didn't like that about me. So it'll be good for you to find out why you're unhappy with yourself."

She nodded. I was happy that she gave me a chance to let her see that I did understand.

"It wasn't until I started liking me and feeling okay about myself that I could stop wanting to be like others. I couldn't expect people to like me if I didn't like myself. Does that sound crazy?"

"No, no, I get it. But I'm asking, how can I change myself?"

"Well, I did it through prayer. I don't know if you believe in Jesus Christ."

She said, "I go to church sometimes and I do pray before I eat my food."

"Well, now you need to pray and ask God to come into

your heart. Maybe it's time you get to know Him. Even when I'm confused about why a good person like Tim is gone, I know that the Lord knows what's best for us. He can help us love ourselves. Just start praying, Greta."

"How do you pray?"

"Talk to God just like you're talking to me. Tell Him whatever is going on with you. I promise you're gonna feel better."

"Girls, I know you two aren't over there talking. You haven't taken one practice test yet," the teacher said as she walked in.

"Thanks, Morgan," she whispered.

We both turned on our computers and got to work. Without even being afraid, I started answering the questions. For the first time, I got 10 out of 10 correct! When I helped someone else, God helped me. My mom was right. Tim was always going to be with me. I was gonna miss my buddy, but I smiled, knowing how proud he would be to see that my screen showed 100 percent.

"We did it, Tim," I said quietly to myself.

And we can do it again, I could imagine him saying.

• • • • •

"Okay, class. We've got one more day before the CRCT," Mrs. Hardy said to us. "And we're going to spend all day reviewing our lessons."

Trey raised his hand. "We gotta spend all day on it, Mrs. Hardy? We've been doin' this stuff all year."

"You are correct. Then we should fly right through these review lessons."

Trey was right. We had studied all year. Mrs. Hardy was also right. It wouldn't hurt to practice some more. I felt like I was ready for the test and then again I wasn't. I had knots in my stomach every time somebody **mentioned** that big test.

"It's time to open the booklets on your desks so we can go over some important tips about the test. I think this will help you be more prepared. Alec, you can begin by reading the definition of the CRCT for us."

"The CRCT is a series of achievement tests **mandated** by the state. It covers the subject areas of English, reading, math, science, and social studies."

"Good job. Billy, please read for us what the CRCT measures."

Billy was looking down with his eyes closed. She went over to him and tapped him with the ruler. The whole class laughed. That was the first time in a long time that we had laughed. It felt good. Trey reached over and pointed in the book where Billy needed to be.

"Oh, the CRCT measures how well students know the lesson material for their grade level. The test tells if students are learning and provides data to schools so that no child is left behind."

"Exactly. This test is to make sure everybody is learning, so don't feel like we're giving it to you to hold you back. The grading is fair to make sure everyone is placed where they need to be. Trey, how is the CRCT scored?"

Trey started reading, "There are four questions labeled A, B, C, and D. Students are to choose an answer for each question. Also, there are three performance levels: 'does not meet standards,' 'meets the standards,' or 'exceeds the standards.'"

"Great. My next question is how can you prepare for the CRCT? Morgan, please read the test-taking strategies."

"Yes, ma'am," I said, as I began to read. "Weeks before the test, students should set goals to prepare for areas of weakness. Students should have a workplace clear of **distractions**. Students should ask questions when they don't understand. At the end of the study session, teachers can answer the questions."

"Okay, but what about the day before the test, Morgan?"

"Students should get a good night's rest. Students should talk to their parents if they're having any kind of anxiety. Students should know that the test is only to measure their knowledge."

Trey raised his hand. "You say that the test only tests our knowledge, but what happens if we don't pass? We can't go on to the next grade?"

"You'll pass. Don't worry. We've been working very hard and it's going to pay off. Morgan, what about the day of the big test?"

"Students should eat a good breakfast. Students should arrive on time. Students should take a deep breath and relax. Students should read through each question carefully. If you do not understand, you should ask the teacher. You should not skip questions. You should go back and check your work. Students should stay calm."

Reading the information actually made me feel better. I was ready to take the CRCT and pass it too.

"Now that we've got that out of the way, we need to know three things about reading. You should read for vocabulary, you need to read with comprehension, and you need to read for information. What does reading for vocabulary mean?"

Billy raised his hand and answered, "It means looking for big words to know and learn."

"Exactly. Also, knowing how to read through paragraphs and understand how to use those words in a sentence. It's important to read all throughout the year. What is reading for comprehension?"

"It means understand what you read," said Brooke, after she raised her hand.

"Correct. And Greta, what is reading for information?"

"Well, it's kinda like comprehension because you want to understand what you're reading and that way you can get more information."

"More to the point, remember when we talked about antonyms and synonyms. Synonyms are words with the same meanings and antonyms are words with opposite meanings. Antonyms: tall and short, big and small. Synonyms: smart and clever, fine and good, start and begin.

You also need to know homophones like *present*, meaning 'a gift' and *present*, meaning 'here' or 'in attendance.' We went over those kinds of words earlier this year. In reading comprehension, you need to **summarize** and find the main points. When reading for information, you should be able to remember what you have read. Class, do you understand?"

"Yes, ma'am."

"We have studied the math, science, social studies, and English skills you will find on the test."

Mrs. Hardy looked out over the class. She could tell by our faces that we were trying to understand everything. Then she said something we were glad to hear, "It's time for lunch, class, and I know that this is a lot to take in, but that's why I'm here. We've gone over everything already but if there is something that you just don't quite get, ask questions. Please. I want you to be confident, but you have to relax your mind. As Morgan read, believe you can. Tomorrow, when you all come in, you will get this. I'm so proud of all of you."

Knowing Mrs. Hardy was proud of us was a good feeling. It was telling me that we were going to do well. She'd been tough on us all year, but for a good cause. We were more than ready. Bring on the test! What was I thinking? I was thinking I could handle it. I just hoped I'd be feeling the same way tomorrow.

• • • • •

Well, the big day had finally arrived! I knew I could do my best, and I wasn't going to talk myself out of it. Mom had made a big breakfast for me: pancakes, scrambled eggs, and bacon that smelled good all over the house. I guess it smelled so good that little Jayden toddled up to tell me so.

"Some, some," he tried to say. He was getting so big.

I had been studying so hard for the CRCT that I didn't realize my baby brother could talk. I promised myself that once this day was over I would spend more time with him. Time was going by and he was growing up so fast.

"Morgan, you know you're going to do great, right?" Mom said to me, giving Jayden a piece of pancake so he wouldn't take any more of mine.

"Yes, ma'am. I'm ready."

"How are you feeling about the test this morning?"

"I feel good. I know that the Lord wouldn't want me to be afraid. I'm going to put all my faith in Him so that I can get really good scores."

"I'll be proud of your results no matter what they are," Mom said, giving me a big hug.

Once we got to school, there was no time to play. All of the teachers were standing on their posts in the hallways, smiling and encouraging us all. It was a great effort by them but each one of us had to take the test for ourselves. I believed we could do it.

I walked into the classroom, put my things away, and sat down at my desk. As soon as I looked up, I saw we had a visitor. It was Tim's mom. It had been a week since Tim had gone to heaven. Though our class had sent her flowers and a big card, none of us had talked to her. She seemed to be doing better now.

"I'm not going to take up too much of your time. I just wanted to stop by and say how thankful I am that my son was in your class. I thought I was going to watch him grow up, but the Lord had a different plan. Last year, I didn't think I'd ever get to see him so happy. He had some tough times, being a special kid and all. But, because of you all, this year, he had friends. He felt like he belonged. He enjoyed coming to school every day."

I was smiling as I listened to Tim's mom. She was being so brave even though she'd just lost her little boy and her husband. As she continued talking, I looked around the room at my classmates and they were smiling too. Mrs. Clark went on to give us the confidence we needed. "He talked about you guys all the time. Alec, Trey, and friend Morgan, as he called her. Your teacher tells me that you miss him too. I want you each to know you're growing up to be a fine person. You're going to do great things and it starts with this test. So relax, know I'm praying for you and that you're **capable**."

I couldn't even stay in my seat. I got up and ran up to hug her so tight. I did miss Tim and I knew she missed him even more. She lost her husband too and here she was telling us that we could make it. She was strong. A true Esther. I pulled back and she looked down at me.

"You're a fine young lady, Morgan. You got over your fear of being buddies with someone who was different. The rest of the class joined in too. You helped change my son's life and I'm thankful for that." Then she left before any of us could cry.

Now it was time to get to work.

The first day was reading. I couldn't say that I got all of the questions right but I did feel sure about most of my answers. After we were done, all of us lined up for recess. When we were out on the playground playing kickball, I couldn't play. I couldn't get thoughts of Tim off my mind. He was here one day and gone the next. His mom had come in and was so sweet to us. I just didn't want to play without him.

I sat down on a swing and made sure the one next to me didn't move. Alec came over and said, "You miss Tim, don't you?"

Trey, Brooke, and Billy were playing nearby. They heard us talking and rushed over. Trey said, "We miss him too."

Greta joined in and said, "We should do something really nice for him . . . something to remember him by."

I jumped up and hugged her. "Greta, that's a great idea! We gotta do something really special to remember Tim by."

Everyone started telling her how exciting her idea was. I could tell that she was happy to be part of our group. More kids from the class joined us and gave some ideas about what we could do. It didn't matter that we couldn't come up with the whole plan right then, but at least we were trying. Tim didn't just have an impact on me. He made us all care about others.

"I was sorry I couldn't go to the funeral service," Trey said. "My dad didn't think it was a good idea."

"Maybe we should just pray," Alec said, looking at me like it was my job.

Greta said, "Yeah, Morgan knows how to pray."

"Okay," I said, as they all waited on me.

"Lord, we miss our friend Tim. We want to do something for him but don't know what. Help us think of something great. Help us not to forget him, because he made us all better just by knowing him. We know that he is safe because he's with You. He's up there on the best playground ever. Help his mom. Help us all. In Jesus' name, I pray. Amen."

At that very moment, a beautiful white bird came soaring above us. The way it was flying around us, it was like he knew all of us. Then we all watched the beautiful bird fly away.

Letter to Dad

Dear Dad,

I've learned that being **sarcastic** is not cool. It will put you on the **outskirts**. I **mentioned** this because I know what it's like not to have friends. I am trying to help people not feel alone.

My teacher has taught me not to sweat the big test. She said I'm prepared and not to let any **distractions** get in my way. But I get nervous because it is a **mandated** test. Since I've studied hard for it, hopefully it'll **summarize** that I do know the standards. I know you'd tell me I can do it because I am **capable**.

Your daughter,
Hopeful Morgan

Word Search

```
A M S M S D T I Z E T L
S O A A T I E G U D H Z
T R R N E S N J E E I Z
R G C M S T C L Z N S P
I A A A T R B W I O I N
K N S N E A O R R I S W
S N T D P C M A A T A O
T O I A H T M P M N G D
U E C T A I A U M E O D
O L F E N O N P U M O N
P L O D I N D J S S D A
D E K R E S M E N T U P
```

CAPABLE

DISTRACTIONS

MANDATED

MENTIONED

OUTSKIRTS

SARCASTIC

SUMMARIZE

Words to Know and Learn

1) sar·cas·tic (sär-kăs'tĭk) *adjective*
A cutting, often ironic remark intended to cause hurt feelings.

2) outskirts (out'skûrt's) *noun*
 Outlying or bordering areas; apart from the main place or group.

3) men·tion (měn'shən) *verb*
men·tioned past tense
To refer to, especially incidentally.

4) dis·trac·tions (dĭ-străk'shəns) *noun*
Something that draws or directs one's attention away.

5) man·da·ted (măn'dāt') *verb* (past tense)
To order or command.

6) sum·ma·rize (sŭm'ə-rīz') *verb*
Present material in a shortened form.

7) ca·pa·ble (kā'pə-bəl) *adjective*
Qualified.

Chapter 7

Beautiful Mind

As the two of us walked into the grocery store, Mom said, "I'm so very proud of you, Morgan."

Giving me a big hug, she said, "Mrs. Hardy called and told me that you took all of your CRCT **sections** and she felt you scored well."

I wasn't nearly as sure as Mrs. Hardy. I mean, I'd done the best I could. I went back over my answers and prayed about it all. I turned it in thinking I did okay, but what if I didn't? What would happen?

"Morgan, why do you have such a long face? What's wrong?" Mom asked me, as she grabbed a cart.

"I just wanna make sure I passed," I said, knowing that she wasn't going to let me give her the "nothing" answer. I had to tell her the truth, and I really was worried.

"Sweetheart, you've got to clear your mind of thoughts like that. Quit being so hard on yourself, and stop thinking that you can't do it. Mrs. Hardy sounded so pleased about your test scores. If she didn't think you had done well, she wouldn't have called. You've got to get a handle on this fear, Morgan or it's going to **consume** you. Now, repeat after me: I can do this."

"I can do this," I said, a little weakly.

"Now, this time say it like you mean it. I can do this." Mom was coaching me loud enough for the whole store to notice us. She didn't care who was watching, she just raised her hands up high in the air like a cheerleader.

"I can do this!" I shouted. "I did my best and that's good enough!"

"See, the more you believe in yourself and trust in God, positive things will happen for you. That's how you handle things."

"Mom, can I get some of my favorite cold cereal?" I asked. I wanted some, but I also wanted to change the subject.

"Sure. As soon as you're done, meet me in the canned vegetable and soup **aisle**."

"Okay, I'm gonna get some oatmeal too."

Walking over to the cereal, my head was down and I knew I had to stop thinking wrong thoughts. So I prayed, *Lord, just help me trust You more. Help me understand that I did the best I could and it's okay. Mama always talks about seeing the glass half full. I need to be more positive like that. I need You, Lord. Amen.*

I raised my head high and finished my prayer. Then I

saw the big, bad Bridget. She wasn't looking at me, so I quickly darted out of the aisle. I didn't get the box of cereal I wanted, but I couldn't go back and face her. The last time I saw her at the court building, she did something that scared me crazy. I got away as quickly as I could.

Thinking I was in the same aisle as my mom, I ended up in the aisle with cake mix and sugar. Bridget was there too. She was looking right at me. She lifted her finger and her mouth said, "Come here." I didn't say a word back. I just followed her direction. Her hand was balled into a fist and I hoped this grocery store had cameras, because if she hit me I wanted it to be on tape.

She could tell I was acting scared, so she said, "What's wrong with you? I saw you run to the other aisle."

"How did you see me?" I said, with my teeth clicking like I was out in the cold.

"I was watchin' you. We need to talk," she said in the same scary voice she used before.

I just stood there. I couldn't move. Was she going to hit me? Was she going to yell at me?

"I wanna tell you I'm sorry."

My eyes got big. "What?" I said before I could hold it in.

"Yeah, you heard me right. The last time I saw you I was pretty mean. I thought that you wanted to be there to tell on me. But later on, I thought about it some more. Even if you did, it would be for the right reason. I did do something bad to you."

"Yeah, you did. But you already told me you were sorry.

I was only there because I had to be. I didn't want to."

"Well, after you left, I was sitting there trying to blame other people for my mistakes. But somethin' told me that wasn't right. I got myself in trouble and now I'm on probation. I've learned a lot from it. It was nobody's fault but mine."

I just stood there listening in surprise as Bridget poured out her heart.

"Next year, I'm going to middle school and I'm determined not to be so mean. I was only actin' out because of the situation with my mom, my brother, and me bouncing around from place to place. I guess I just got tired of it. Then I saw you had everything that I wanted and it just didn't seem fair. So I just took what I wanted. Now I know that was the wrong thing to do and I'm sorry."

"Bridget, I accepted your apology the first time. You just need to know that I've got problems too."

"Come on," she said, not believing me.

"I don't know if Billy told you or not, but my dad is in the Navy and he's far away. I haven't seen him in almost two years. Then last month, a naval ship was shot up."

"Oh, no! That was your dad's ship?"

"No! I'm so happy it wasn't. But it could've been."

"You've gotta stay positive. You can't go around thinkin' somethin' bad will happen to him."

"You're right, Bridget. Thanks for that."

"I guess you never really know what's goin' on with other people. Here, I think you wanted these." She handed me a box of my favorite cereal.

"How did you know?"

"When you saw me, you were reachin' for this one and then you dropped it and ran."

"You're real cool, Bridget," I said to her.

"I'm working on it. I just keep tellin' myself that I'm gonna be a better person."

"I'm doin' the same thing, girl. I think we just need to keep leanin' on God for faith and strength and we'll both be better."

We nodded together.

● ● ● ● ●

I was out on the playground, looking at the pretty flowers. They're lined up in rows along the side of the school building. I remember when Tim picked one and gave it to me. It was only a buttercup, but it meant a lot to him and to me. I just didn't want to be sad thinking about him, so I was trying my best to smile.

Alec came over to me. "Hey. What's goin' on? You still thinkin' about the CRCT? Morgan, you know you passed. Stop worrying."

"I think I did too. You mean, you're not worried about it just a little bit?" I asked him.

"No. If I didn't do so well on any part, I'd just have to take it over again. It's not that big of a deal, Morgan. I have more important things goin' on in my house than for me to be worried about some test."

I wanted to ask what was going on, but I didn't want to be nosy. I felt if he wanted me to know, he would tell me. He knew I was here if he wanted to talk.

"Okay, so if you weren't thinkin' about the test, what's on your mind?"

"I remember when Tim picked me some flowers. I was just missing him, that's all."

"That's it, Morgan!"

"What's it?" I asked him.

"You got the idea! Hey, everybody, come over here!" Alec called out to our classmates. "Morgan just thought of what we can do to remember Tim."

"I did?" I couldn't imagine what he was talking about.

"Yeah. We can make him a garden with lots of colorful flowers. It shouldn't be any trouble for parents to bring some plants for us. We can get our teacher to bring some soil. And I'll get my dad to make a **plaque** with Tim's name on it. It'll be cool. You'll see."

"Yeah," said Trey. "Plus, we'll be digging up the soil. That's science and Mrs. Hardy will love that."

When recess was over, the whole class couldn't wait to line up. We were ready to go inside and tell Mrs. Hardy the good news about our idea for Tim. This was going to be a blast. I pulled Alec to the side.

"You didn't have to say that it was my idea, because it wasn't. It was all you."

"No, you're the one who knew what Tim liked to do. It was you."

"But I didn't think about the garden."

"You thought about the garden," he said.

"Ugh, Alec," I said, not wanting credit for something he thought of.

"Ugh, Morgan. Then it was both of us, okay?"

"Okay," I said, giving in because Alec was so cool.

It was a pretty cool thing we could do to honor Tim. He was a terrific boy.

When I went home that afternoon, I told Mom all about Tim's garden. She thought it was a great idea too. Mom said she was willing to help out in any way I needed her.

When we told our teacher about it, Mrs. Hardy also loved the plan. She was thrilled and ready to get started right away. The next day, we started an all-school project. By Friday, we had flowers coming from everywhere. The kindergarten class all the way through the fifth grade brought something we could plant.

Alec's dad had an awesome sign made. It was a fancy black plaque made of shiny metal.

"It looks like it has lights on it," said Trey, when Alec showed it to us.

"It really does. It's beautiful," I replied.

"It's **solar**," Alec explained. "At night it'll be able to light up and Tim's name will be shining for everyone to see. Maybe he can even see it from heaven."

Just then Greta walked up with a bunch of cards in her hand. Not saying anything, she just stood there, looking at all of us.

Billy was rude to her. "If you're gonna hand them out, just do it already."

After giving him a not-too-happy look, I asked Greta, "What's wrong?"

As Greta slowly started passing out her invitations, she told me, "I don't think anyone wants to come to my party. And I don't want them to come if they don't want to." I could tell that she was really worried about it.

"Greta, if people don't come to your party, too bad for them. I know I'm gonna be there, so it can be just us two. But I know those guys in our class. Anytime you say the words party, snacks, treats, ice cream, or cake, they'll come."

"You really think so?"

I nodded and gave her a big smile.

"I didn't get one," Billy said.

"And where's mine?" Brooke asked.

Greta finally finished passing out her cards and we all opened them up.

"See ya in two weeks!" said Alec, making a funny joke.

"I know I'm comin'," said Trey.

I was so happy that I hugged Greta. "See how wonderful this is? You put it out there and people wanna come."

"Thanks for bein' so nice, Morgan," she said to me.

"What do you mean?"

"I know my party's gonna be cool now!"

Later that day, the principal called everyone out of the school. It was almost like a fire drill but it wasn't. She wanted everyone to see the beautiful garden we made for Tim. Dr. Sharpe read aloud to everyone a sign made in his honor: "In Memory of Tim Clark. If you open your heart to the good things in life, you can create lovely things."

• • • • •

I was on the bus and I couldn't wait to get home and show Mom my CRCT results. Mrs. Hardy said they were outstanding and I knew Mom would say that I had worried for nothing. But, I was learning to put my worries in God's hands. I was glad that the whole class passed too. Mrs. Hardy taught us so much, we studied hard all year, and it really paid off.

Alec had the highest scores in the whole class. But you wouldn't know it the way he was sitting on the bus, looking like he had failed. I promised myself I'd stay out of his business, but he was my buddy.

I tapped him on the shoulder and said, "Hey, what's goin' on with you?"

Sure enough, he gave me the answer I usually give my mom. "Nothing."

"No, don't say that. You're always the one trying to cheer me up and giving me good advice. And I know somethin' is wrong with you."

"I just don't wanna go home, that's all."

"Why not? Your parents are gonna be excited when they see your marks."

"My parents haven't been happy about too many

things lately. Things haven't been going so well. Hey, Morgan, when your parents got a divorce, how did you deal with it?"

"Well, first of all, you don't even know that your parents are gonna get a divorce."

"Don't try and **minimize** the problem," he snapped back. "You don't hear all the yelling and screaming that goes on in my house."

"Okay, I'm sorry. It was almost three years ago, but I remember like it was yesterday. None of the arguing felt good to hear. I hope you're not havin' to go through any of that."

"I'm not tryin' to be mean with you or anything, Morgan. Just forget it. You can't help me."

"No, really, Alec. You told me that you like the fact that I have somethin' you wanted. Right? Like I believe in God and I talk to Him and stuff?"

"Yeah."

"Well, now I've accepted Him in my heart."

"Really?"

"Yeah. I took the next step. I still have a lot to learn. I need to know His Word so I can grow. Now I know that I'm not supposed to be afraid. Just like with the CRCT. Alec, you said you had bigger problems to worry about. And I'm thinkin' that it must be your parents."

I could tell that he was listening, and I had more to say to him. "But you know, Alec, we're not supposed to worry about anything. I learned in Sunday school that we're supposed to give all of our cares to God. He can take care of our problems better than we can. So keep praying for your parents. Keep praying for better days to come. God will hear you. Over the last two years, I've grown a lot. And I know that God is on my side. So, go home smiling and believing. Everything is gonna be all right."

"Thanks, Morgan," he said, sort of smiling. Somehow I knew he was going to give it a try.

When we arrived at our stop, of course, Alec's brother, Antoine, dashed past us to get off the bus. As he ran past me, I felt him tap me on the back of my head. I'm so glad Alec is nothing like him.

"Sorry about that," Alec said, apologizing for his brother.

"It's okay, it didn't hurt. I'll see you later."

"You bet."

As I walked up our front stairs, Mom was standing there with the door open.

"We got an e-mail. CRCT results are in."

"Look at them, Mom!"

Reading the scores on my paper, she said with joy and a little relief, "Oh, my goodness, Morgan! You excelled in reading and math!"

"Yes, Mom! I'm so excited! I'm going to the fourth grade. Yay!"

"That is so wonderful, baby. We have to go out and celebrate. This is a special day. Come on in and get dressed, honey. Put on that new dress I laid on your bed."

"You bought me a new dress? You mean, you already knew?"

"Well, I just had a feeling you did great."

Feeling extra special, I said, "Thanks, Mom!"

On the way to my room, I saw Daddy Derek walking through the hallway with my baby brother. "Hi, little Jayden! Hey, Daddy Derek!" I said, as happy as I could be.

"Hey, Morgan. Did somebody do well on their CRCT?"

"Yes, I did!"

"Well then, let's get ready to celebrate. We have a big surprise for you because this is a big deal."

I got dressed so fast I almost forgot to zip my dress. I was just imagining the fancy restaurant we were going to. We loaded into the car and took off. After riding for a while, we passed a sign that read AIRPORT.

I wondered, *What does an airport have to do with eating?*

It wasn't a big Atlanta airport either. It seemed much smaller and more private.

"Where are we going, Mom?"

She just smiled and wouldn't say a thing. As soon as we parked, I saw kids holding signs that read, "Welcome home, Mom!" and "Welcome home, Dad!" Then I saw a lot of USA flags and naval officers in their uniforms.

"We'd better hurry and get inside," Mom said.

"No way," I whispered, thinking it could be what I was hoping it would be.

"Yes, way," Mom said.

We got to the **base** just in time to see the large plane land. Camera crews were there filming the action as the doors to the plane opened. To my surprise, the first person off of the plane was my dad, Officer Monty Love! He was carrying a big, purple teddy bear almost the size of me in his arms. My dad was back!

I ran up to him, yelling, "Daddy! Daddy! Daddy! You're safe! I missed you!"

Then, wrapping my arms around him as he scooped me up in his arms, I couldn't stop kissing him and telling him, "I love you so much!"

"Morgan, baby, I missed you more and I'm glad you're safe," he said as he swung me around.

I just couldn't stop crying. All the nights I wanted him to be okay. All the times I needed him to hug me tight. All the times I just wanted to see his face. Well, that time was here! I couldn't ask for a better reward for passing the CRCT.

"Thank You, God!" I yelled out.

After putting me back down on the ground, my dad walked over to Daddy Derek and shook his hand. "Thank you for taking care of my little girl," Dad said.

Daddy Derek said, "You're welcome, man. And thank you for taking care of us."

Then, turning to Mom, he said, "You've done well with her. Our daughter is so beautiful."

There was a special dinner for the servicemen and women and their families. We all attended because we're one big family. My dad couldn't stop looking at me and I couldn't take my eyes off of him.

I was so proud to sit next to Dad and he was so proud of me. "Thank you, Morgan, for all your letters. I learned so much about you. You've grown so much. You've got the right mind. You've got the right spirit. And you've got God."

Looking around the table with so much emotion on his face, Dad said to all of us, "God brought me back to Morgan. God is awesome, isn't He?"

"Yes, He is," we all agreed.

Then I said, "I was scared, Dad. I was scared I wouldn't ever see you again. I was scared I wouldn't pass my test. I was scared about dying."

"You're not scared anymore, are you, baby?"

"No, sir! I know God has been taking care of us and He loves me. I just have to keep listening and following His Word. And I have to keep doing good so I can go far. Most of all, I have to keep God in my heart."

"Look at my Morgan. You're growing up. You're beautiful on the inside and on the outside. I am so proud of you because you've got your head on straight. You have a beautiful mind."

Letter to Dad

Dear Dad,

You're back! And all the **sections** in my body are happy to see you. Thoughts of you being **safe consume** me. Seeing you walk down the **aisle** in the airport made my world a better place.

We made a **plaque** with a **solar** light for Tim. I don't want anything to **minimize** my time with you. And I was so glad to see you at the **base**. I'm never letting you go.

Your daughter,
Overjoyed Morgan

Word Search

```
N  T  O  G  E  T  H  S  E  R  V  E
O  B  H  L  J  I  E  G  O  P  H  A
W  E  S  G  O  C  D  A  B  L  Z  R
B  I  A  M  T  K  O  X  S  O  A  P
A  Z  R  I  C  T  G  N  J  C  F  R
S  L  O  N  F  O  Y  E  S  D  E  S
E  N  D  I  N  C  M  B  W  U  T  R
S  X  O  M  A  K  U  L  Q  P  M  A
H  A  W  I  C  N  R  A  U  T  A  E
A  B  N  Z  K  F  L  M  R  K  V  B
V  C  H  E  I  P  W  Y  A  T  T  I
E  O  R  I  F  I  N  I  S  H  E  D
```

AISLE

BASE

CONSUME

MINIMIZE

PLAQUE

SECTIONS

SOLAR

Words to Know and Learn

1) sec·tion (sĕk'shən) *noun*
One of several components; a piece.

2) con·sume (kən-sūm') *verb*
To take in as food; eat or drink up.

3) aisle (īl) *noun*
A passageway for inside traffic, as in a store.

4) plaque (plăk) *noun*
A flat plate with writing on it.

5) so·lar (sō'lər) *adjective*
Having to do with the sun.

6) min·i·mize (mĭn'ə-mīz') *verb*
To make seem less important.

7) base (bās) *noun*
A central location, such as a military base.

Morgan Love Series: Book 5

No Fear!

Stephanie Perry Moore
Discussion Questions

1. Mrs. Hardy, Morgan's teacher, explains the importance of the class passing the upcoming mandatory standard test. Do you think since Morgan is a good student that she should be worried about the test? How do you feel when it's time to take a big exam?

2. Tim, the special needs student, is brought to Mrs. Hardy's room to be a part of her class. Do you think Morgan was right to welcome him? What do you do when you have to make friends with someone who seems different?

3. Morgan doesn't do well on a practice test. She is not happy because she has to get after-school tutoring help. How do you think Morgan should have approached the tutoring sessions? What would you do if you didn't know something related to your schoolwork?

4. Morgan learns that a naval ship has been attacked. She gets fearful right away, thinking about her dad's safety. Do you think jumping to conclusions is a good idea? When something frightening happens, do you pray to the Lord for help?

5. There is a bad storm that takes place in the town. The kids learn that Tim and his father were in a fatal car accident. How do you think the class felt about this news? What do you think about heaven?

6. Morgan finally learns that the Lord doesn't want her to fear and she takes her test with confidence. Do you think she finally had the right attitude about the big test? How do you get over your fears?

7. Morgan missed her dad so much. How do you think she felt when she finally saw him again? What things are you thankful for?

Word Keep Book

Chapter 1: flicked, competency, precedence, anxiety, plastered, persuaded, scenarios

Chapter 2: ignorance, sporadic, exposed, isolated, anxious, denominators, possessive

Chapter 3: excel, refined, devastated, subpoena, exchange, grip, brutal

Chapter 4: implementing, intentionally, dynamic, barricade, chitchat, commotion, exhaled

Chapter 5: occurring, tragically, impact, petrified, retaliation, probation, salvation

Chapter 6: sarcastic, outskirts, mentioned, distractions, mandated, summarize, capable

Chapter 7: sections, consume, aisle, plaque, solar, minimize, base

4 Bonus Math Pages

Worksheet 1: Adding Like Denominators

Instructions: To add like denominators, keep the bottom number the same and add the top two numbers. Then reduce if you can. If the number on the top is more than the bottom number, then you must simplify.

Example: $\dfrac{5}{12} + \dfrac{3}{12} = \dfrac{8}{12}$ but this number can be reduced to $\dfrac{2}{3}$

Or

$\dfrac{6}{10} + \dfrac{7}{10} = \dfrac{13}{10}$ but 13 is larger than 10. Ten goes into 13 one time with 3 left over.

Answer: $1\dfrac{3}{10}$

1) $\dfrac{4}{10} + \dfrac{2}{10} =$ 2) $\dfrac{2}{8} + \dfrac{1}{8} =$ 3) $\dfrac{4}{10} + \dfrac{6}{10} =$

4) $\dfrac{1}{12} + \dfrac{2}{12} =$ 5) $\dfrac{2}{12} + \dfrac{6}{12} =$ 6) $\dfrac{3}{12} + \dfrac{2}{12} =$

7) $\dfrac{8}{11} + \dfrac{3}{11} =$ 8) $\dfrac{7}{9} + \dfrac{2}{9} =$ 9) $\dfrac{3}{12} + \dfrac{11}{12} =$

10) $\dfrac{1}{11} + \dfrac{4}{11} =$ 11) $\dfrac{1}{11} + \dfrac{8}{11} =$ 12) $\dfrac{3}{7} + \dfrac{1}{7} =$

Worksheet 2: Number Counting

Instructions: Starting at 1200, skip-count by 100, and fill in the missing numbers.

Example: 1200,_____, 1400,_____, 1600,_____, _____

Answers: 1300, 1500, 1700 and 1800

			1500				
			2300				
	2900			3200			
		3800					
	4500				4900	5000	5100
		5400					5900
			6300				
	6900					7400	

Worksheet 3: Missing Place Values

Instructions: Look at the digits and add them up. (Mental math can help if you put them in order by place value.)

Example: 200 + 40 + 10000 + 2 + 6000 = 16242
(Put in order for 10000 + 6000 + 200 + 40 + 2)

1. 3000 + 100 + 80 + 1 + 10000 = _____

2. 30 + 10000 + 600 + 5000 + 8 = _____

3. 4 + 60 + 800 + 4000 + 80000 = _____

4. 9 + 30 + 700 + 30000 = _____

5. 6 + 100 + 80 + 60000 = _____

6. 700 + 70 + 10000 + 4000 + 2 = _____

7. 1 + 80 + 600 + 2000 + 20000 = _____

8. 7 + 700 + 9000 + 10000 + 80 = _____

9. 30000 + 600 + 40 + 2000 + 4 = _____

10. 1 + 600 + 10 + 20000 = _____

Worksheet 4: Measuring

Instructions: Convert the measuring units as indicated.

Example: 5 pt, 0 c = _____ c

Answer: 10 c

Example: 14 qt = _____ gal _____ qt

Answer: 3 gal, 2 qt

1. 4 qt, 0 pt = _____ pt

2. 1 gal, 1 qt = _____ qt

3. 27 qt = _____ gal _____ qt

4. 9 yd, 1 ft = _____ ft

5. 2 pt = _____ qt _____ pt

6. 0 qt, 1 pt = _____ pt

7. 6 pt, 0 c = _____ c

8. 3 pt, 0 c = _____ c

9. 1 c = _____ qt _____ c

10. 7 lb, 4 oz = _____ oz

11. 93 in = _____ ft _____ in

12. 17 qt = _____ gal _____ qt

Chapter 1 Solution

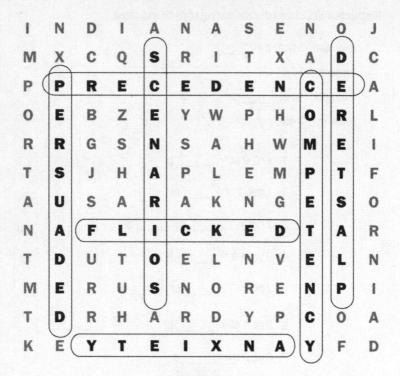

```
I  N  D  I  A  N  A  S  E  N  O  J
M  X  C  Q  S  R  I  T  X  A  D  C
P  P  R  E  C  E  D  E  N  C  E  A
O  E  B  Z  E  Y  W  P  H  O  R  L
R  R  G  S  N  S  A  H  W  M  E  I
T  S  J  H  A  P  L  E  M  P  T  F
A  U  S  A  R  A  K  N  G  E  S  O
N  A  F  L  I  C  K  E  D  T  A  R
T  D  U  T  O  E  L  N  V  E  L  N
M  E  R  U  S  N  O  R  E  N  P  I
T  D  R  H  A  R  D  Y  P  C  O  A
K  E  Y  T  E  I  X  N  A  Y  F  D
```

ANXIETY

COMPETENCY

FLICKED

PERSUADED

PLASTERED

PRECEDENCE

SCENARIOS

Chapter 2 Solution

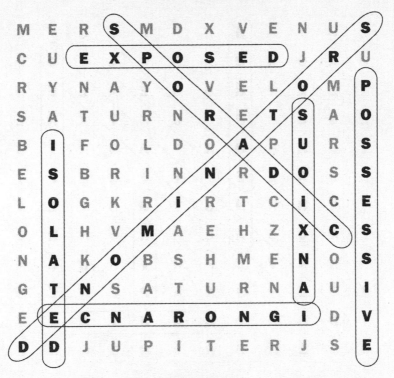

ANXIOUS

DENOMINATORS

EXPOSED

IGNORANCE

ISOLATED

POSSESSIVE

SPORADIC

Chapter 3 Solution

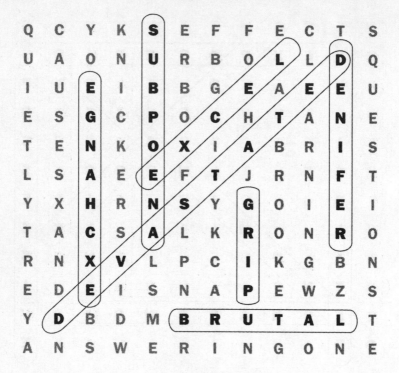

```
Q  C  Y  K  S  E  F  F  E  C  T  S
U  A  O  N  U  R  B  O  L  L  D  Q
I  U  E  I  B  B  G  E  A  E  E  U
E  S  G  C  P  O  C  H  T  A  N  E
T  E  N  K  O  X  I  A  B  R  I  S
L  S  A  E  E  F  T  J  R  N  F  T
Y  X  H  R  N  S  Y  G  O  I  E  I
T  A  C  S  A  L  K  R  O  N  R  O
R  N  X  V  L  P  C  I  K  G  B  N
E  D  E  I  S  N  A  P  E  W  Z  S
Y  D  B  D  M  B  R  U  T  A  L  T
A  N  S  W  E  R  I  N  G  O  N  E
```

BRUTAL

DEVASTATED

EXCEL

EXCHANGE

GRIP

REFINED

SUBPOENA

Chapter 4 Solution

```
I  B  S  H  A  R  P  E  N  Z  B  X
M  A  X  J  C  H  I  T  C  H  A  T
P  R  A  Q  D  A  P  B  O  S  R  M
L  C  T  D  R  R  E  A  M  C  R  O
E  O  W  E  A  D  R  R  M  H  I  R
M  D  A  L  M  Y  R  N  O  O  C  G
E  E  T  A  A  N  Y  E  T  O  A  A
N  B  E  H  T  R  E  Y  I  L  D  N
T  O  R  X  L  A  M  O  O  R  E  D
I  N  T  E  N  T  I  O  N  A  L  N
N  P  A  U  L  D  Y  N  A  M  I  C
G  S  T  E  P  H  A  N  I  E  Z  F
```

BARRICADE

CHITCHAT

COMMOTION

DYNAMIC

EXHALED

IMPLEMENTING

INTENTIONAL

Chapter 5 Solution

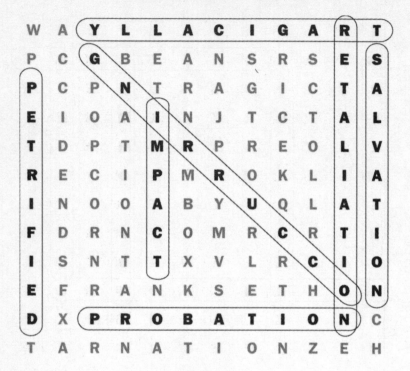

IMPACT

OCCURRING

PETRIFIED

PROBATION

RETALIATION

SALVATION

TRAGICALLY

Chapter 6 Solution

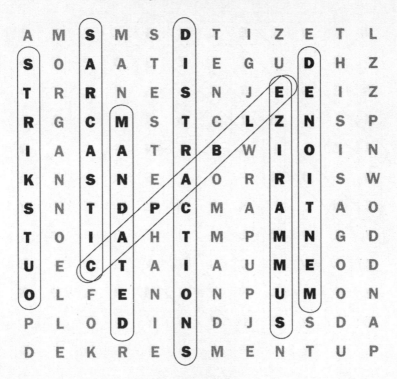

CAPABLE

DISTRACTIONS

MANDATED

MENTIONED

OUTSKIRTS

SARCASTIC

SUMMARIZE

Chapter 7 Solution

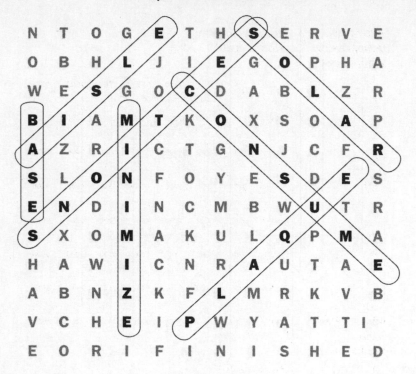

```
N   T   O   G   E   T   H   S   E   R   V   E
O   B   H   L   J   I   E   G   O   P   H   A
W   E   S   G   O   C   D   A   B   L   Z   R
B   I   A   M   T   K   O   X   S   O   A   P
A   Z   R   I   C   T   G   N   J   C   F   R
S   L   O   N   F   O   Y   E   S   D   E   S
E   N   D   I   N   C   M   B   W   U   T   R
S   X   O   M   A   K   U   L   Q   P   M   A
H   A   W   I   C   N   R   A   U   T   A   E
A   B   N   Z   K   F   L   M   R   K   V   B
V   C   H   E   I   P   W   Y   A   T   T   I
E   O   R   I   F   I   N   I   S   H   E   D
```

AISLE

BASE

CONSUME

MINIMIZE

PLAQUE

SECTIONS

SOLAR

Answer Keys

Adding Like Denominators Worksheet 1

1. 3/5
2. 3/8
3. 1
4. 1/4
5. 2/3
6. 5/12
7. 1
8. 1
9. 1-1/6
10. 5/11
11. 9/11
12. 4/7

Missing Place Values Worksheet 3

1. 13181
2. 15638
3. 84864
4. 30739
5. 60186
6. 14772
7. 22681
8. 19787
9. 32644
10. 20611

Number Counting Worksheet 2

1200	1300	1400	1500	1600	1700	1800	1900
2000	2100	2200	2300	2400	2500	2600	2700
2800	2900	3000	3100	3200	3300	3400	3500
3600	3700	3800	3900	4000	4100	4200	4300
4400	4500	4600	4700	4800	4900	5000	5100
5200	5300	5400	5500	5600	5700	5800	5900
6000	6100	6200	6300	6400	6500	6600	6700
6800	6900	7000	7100	7200	7300	7400	7500

Measuring Worksheet 4

1. 8 pt
2. 5 qt
3. 6 gal, 3 qt
4. 28 ft
5. 1 qt, 0 pt
6. 1 pt
7. 12 c
8. 6 c
9. 0 qt, 1 c
10. 116 oz
11. 7 ft, 9 in
12. 4 gal, 1 qt

Acknowledgments

So I caught my daughter on the phone when she was NOT supposed to be on it. She'd already made a bad decision to chat when she shouldn't have been on the phone, then when I asked her about it she wanted to tell a fib. She knew admitting the truth would land her in deep trouble, but she also knew telling me an untruth would be much, much worse.

Thankfully, she was smart and did the right thing and admitted her mistake. We talked about her bad choice. I hope she has learned to not disobey and is off punishment by the time you read this. The point is, we all make mistakes. We all get tempted to take the easy way out. We all think from time to time that it is better to act on wrong choices.

However, the Bible is God's law. He expects His people to obey Him. Your parents may seem harsh sometimes, but they do what they do because they have your best interest at heart. So tell them you love them, study hard, be sweet, and keep on making right choices.

I made a right choice to allow great people to help me write for you.

To my parents, Dr. Franklin and Shirley Perry, I want to say thank you for doing the right thing by raising me God's way.

For my Moody/Lift Every Voice Team, especially Roslyn Jordan, I want to say thank you for knowing that the right thing to do in pushing this book is a great marketing strategy.

For my sweet cousin and assistant, Ciara Roundtree, and my brother and his family, Dennis Perry, Leslie Perry, and Franklin Perry, I want to say thank you for giving me your time and always being there.

For my friends who gave input into this series, Sarah Lundy, Jenell Clark, Vanessa Davis Griggs, Carol Hardy, Lois Hardy, Veronica Evans, Sophia Nelson, Laurie Weaver, Taiwanna Brown-Bolds, Lakeba Williams, Jackie Dixon, Vickie Davis, Kim Monroe, Jan Hatchett, Veida Evans, Toi Willis, and Deborah Bradley, I want to say thank you so much for saying the right thing by giving me correct advice.

For my children, Dustyn Leon, Sydni Derek, and Sheldyn Ashli, I want to say thank you for doing the right thing and obeying your dad and me.

For my husband, Derrick Moore, I want to say thank you for doing the right thing by working hard for our family.

For my new young readers, I want to say thank you for doing the right thing by taking time to read, learn, and grow.

And to my Savior Jesus Christ, I want to say thank You for choosing to do the right thing by dying on the cross for all our sins.

A+ ATTITUDE

ISBN-13: 978-0-8024-2263-7

Morgan is mad at the world because she can't have things her way. If she received a grade for her attitude it would be an F. When her mommy gets really sick Morgan realizes how mean she's been. She makes up her mind to have an A+ attitude no matter what.

LiftEveryVoiceBooks.com
MoodyPublishers.com

SPEAK UP

ISBN-13: 978-0-8024-2264-4

Morgan is not sure what to do when she discovers that Alec, the new kid, is bullying her cousin and kids at school. She becomes worried when her friend Trey starts hanging out with and acting like Alec. When Trey brings a knife to school, Morgan decides to speak up.

LiftEveryVoiceBooks.com
MoodyPublishers.com

RIGHT THING

ISBN-13: 978-0-8024-2266-8

When Morgan decides not to follow her mommy's instructions one too many times, she gets in trouble and she gets hurt. When she hears her stepdad Derek talking about the Ten Commandments, she learns that when she disobeys she is not only letting her parents down but God too.

LiftEveryVoiceBooks.com
MoodyPublishers.com

SOMETHING SPECIAL

ISBN-13: 978-0-8024-2265-1

After getting in trouble for teasing her classmates at school and disappointing her parents, Morgan goes to vacation Bible school and learns that God made each person the way they are for a reason. She realizes that she and even those kids she'd teased at school are all okay just the way they are because God made them, and to Him they are all something special.

LiftEveryVoiceBooks.com
MoodyPublishers.com

MAKING THE TEAM

ISBN-13: 978-0-8024-0411-4

The Alec London Series is a series written for youth, 8-12 years old. Alec London is introduced in Stephanie Perry Moore's previously released series, **The Morgan Love Series**. In this new series, readers get a glimpse of Alec's life up close and personal. The series provides moral lessons that will aid in character development, teaching youth, especially boys, how to effectively deal with the various issues they face at this stage of life. The series will also help youth develop their English and math skills as they read through the stories and complete the entertaining and educational exercises provided at the end of each chapter and in the back of the book.

L E V B
LIFT EVERY VOICE BOOKS
LiftEveryVoiceBooks.com
MoodyPublishers.com

OTHER BOOKS IN THE SERIES:

LEARNING THE RULES
GOING THE DISTANCE
WINNING THE BATTLE
TAKING THE LEAD

Lift Every Voice Books

Lift every voice and sing
Till earth and heaven ring,
Ring with the harmonies of Liberty;
Let our rejoicing rise
High as the listening skies,
Let it resound loud as the rolling sea.
Sing a song full of the faith that the dark past has taught us,
Sing a song full of the hope that the present has brought us,
Facing the rising sun of our new day begun
Let us march on till victory is won.

The Black National Anthem, written by James Weldon Johnson in 1900, captures the essence of Lift Every Voice Books. Lift Every Voice Books is an imprint of Moody Publishers that celebrates a rich culture and great heritage of faith, based on the foundation of eternal truth—God's Word. We endeavor to restore the fabric of the African-American soul and reclaim the indomitable spirit that kept our forefathers true to God in spite of insurmountable odds.

We are Lift Every Voice Books—Christ-centered books and resources for restoring the African-American soul.

For more information on other books and products written and produced from a biblical perspective, go to www.lifteveryvoicebooks.com or write to:

Lift Every Voice Books
820 N. LaSalle Boulevard
Chicago, IL 60610
www.lifteveryvoicebooks.com